Sign up for our newsletter to hear
about new and upcoming releases.

www.ylva-publishing.com

OTHER BOOKS IN THE SUPERHEROINE COLLECTION

Shattered
by Lee Winter

COMING:

The Shadow Hand
by Sacchie Green

More books coming in 2018

THE POWER OF MERCY

FIONA ZEDDE

Ylva
THE
SUPERHEROINE
COLLECTION

CHAPTER 1

MAI STOOD ON THE ROOF of the twenty-story building, naked except for the cloak of her restlessness. Faint pain throbbed in her back—scratches from the anonymous woman she'd taken to bed barely two hours before—her thighs ached from the work she'd put into bringing them both pleasure, and the muscles in her arms still burned. The city of Atlanta, studded in starlight above and in bright lights below, hummed its particular late-night songs. A whisper of street traffic. A distant chopper. The thumping bass line from a rap song as a car cruised past.

The woman she'd gone home with still slept peacefully in her bed one flight below, but that same peace escaped Mai. Earlier that night, a familiar restlessness had pushed her into her favorite local bar, a place dark enough for private pleasures yet with a wide-open patio for fresh air and a bar well-stocked enough to drown even the deepest of sorrows. But she didn't go there for sorrow or for fresh air.

The woman she found wasn't exactly what she craved, but in that moment, with familiar demons pulling at her, the lush form with a head full of springy coils had been enough. She tasted like forgetfulness, pain subsumed, pleasure without the consequence of a tomorrow. Starved for what the stranger had offered, Mai had devoured her—the wet flesh between her thighs, her mouth gasping and plush, her breasts like summer-ripe mangoes.

But afterward, Mai was still keyed up. Tight. The big muscles in her arms and thighs jumped just under her skin, ticking away the moments toward an implosion she didn't want to happen. She rolled her shoulders and stretched her neck, spread out her senses to feel what was going on in the city below. It all rushed up to her in a wave of sound and color:

Couples whispering intimately to each other while their bedsheets beneath them rustled to the rhythm of their lovemaking. A police car roaring down the city streets with sirens screaming and blue lights ablaze. Even young children were awake and playing in a nearby courtyard, which was odd for the early fall, when schools were in session. And it was more and more of the same, in a rolling tide of awareness of murder, sex, cruelty, and laughter. The tapestry of a large city.

Mai felt it all, the ceaseless movement of Atlanta—a wild organism in constant flux that could not be tamed. All these things unfolding below her were too far away or too late for her to change. Other things... Mai tilted her head toward the sound of screams pulsing beneath her conscious hearing.

Screams of terror.

A fire.

Mai's breath hitched, and her body unconsciously swayed toward that blast of heat barely two miles away. She narrowed her gaze toward the fire, sharpening her hearing. No sirens headed toward it. Not yet. She wasted a moment wishing for the phone she'd left in the pocket of her discarded jacket somewhere on the stranger's floor. Then she jumped.

Air rushed up to meet her, a gust over her face and bare body, both cooling and heating her as the adrenaline turned her body temperature all the way up to scalding. Everything was loud. Screams rang like church bells, and her body throbbed to the heat radiating from the out-of-control fire.

Falling, Mai grabbed for the stone façade of the next building as it surged up to meet her, bare inches from slamming into her if she miscalculated her headlong rush. She was far from invulnerable, but sometimes it was that vulnerability to death that made these risks worth it.

Closer to the fire, her body tingled, a flush of heat and excitement. She sprinted across a flat roof. Jumped to another.

She flew past a couple pressed together on a blanket, the girl's blouse off, her pert breasts showing, her lover intent on mouthing between her spread thighs.

"Jesus! Did you see that?"

"What?" Her lover emerged, face wet, eyes only for the woman beneath her.

"A naked chick. She just ran past us."

Naked. Right. Mai shifted, felt her skin ripple, hardening and stretching in places. It was only a surface change. She still felt the wind as it brushed her bare skin. Contrary to the illusion she crafted, her hands were gloveless as she grabbed the next rooftop and slung herself over an angled flagpole. There was no sleek catsuit covering her from neck to toe. No high boots. And no mask over the top half of her face, hiding everything but the tight line of her mouth. Any potential witnesses would see what she wanted them to see, not a naked woman streaking across the Atlanta skyline, treating it like her personal sorority house.

Instead, she was Mercy.

Face masked. Body covered. No secrets exposed.

She ran on toward the fire, sliding down into back alleys and darkened side streets when she ran out of roofs, the curse of living in a city with such a jagged and unpredictable skyline. Soon she was close enough to feel the flames, like invisible tongues lapping at her skin. The building was a new construction. Tall and flammable, tempting for any pyromaniac. She could smell the deliberately set fire. Probably someone who was just curious, then shocked when it all went wrong so quickly. She smelled the accelerant and the melting plastic from a disposable lighter, their scents overlaid with panicked sweat and regret.

The building was glorious. Yellow and amber flames swirled in its corners and crevices, holding it tight like a too-ardent lover. Mai took it in all in an instant—the shouts of panic and ringing alarm bells, people hanging out of the smoking mouths of open windows, their whispered or shouted prayers for deliverance.

She listened, dropped to the ground, and ran, her feet pounding the pavement, then leaped UP! Heat lashed her skin, and it was hard not to let it touch her and do what it wanted. The outer wall of the building was hot under her hands and feet.

"Mercy!" someone cried from below. Then a chant rose up—a sound of relief, a sigh, and praise. Just as with the flames, she had to pull herself away from the seduction of the name they had given her. The lure of their raised voices.

A child perched on a window ledge, eyes wide with terror but more afraid of falling the seven stories than of the fire eating his room, bit by relentless bit. Outside the room and screaming in terror, a woman—his mother, Mai guessed—was trying to break down the door. The woman rammed it with a wooden chair already on fire, trying to get to the boy. Smoke choked the woman and the entire apartment. Already she was weakening, nearly passed out from the smoke.

Mai jumped through a nearby window and fought her way into the apartment. She grabbed the woman.

"No! My son!" She whirled at Mai, fighting to stay in the fire, her fist slamming into Mai's face. Mai winced but bore the pain. A whip of flame lashed against her back, and she hissed, protecting the woman from the fire even as her own skin burned. The pain of it was oddly sweet.

Mai grabbed the woman's arms and pinned them behind her back. "I'll get him next if you calm down." She didn't shout. "If you don't stop fighting me, I won't be able to get him."

The woman stilled at once, and Mai threw her over her shoulder, covered her head with a wet towel she'd grabbed from the bathroom on the way in, and sprinted the way she'd come, with the woman's weight bouncing halfway down her back.

She rushed through the fire and out the window and dropped the woman across the street among the gathered crowd.

"Ty! Get my son!" The woman stumbled back toward the building, but her neighbors grabbed her.

4

Mai quickly assessed the fire, listened for the signs of life still in the building. A woman on a higher floor was in danger of suffocating in her closet. An older couple clung together even higher up and fading fast. Mai ran toward a nearby building miraculously free of the blaze, scaled its outer wall, and leapt from it to the flame-enshrouded condo complex.

She quickly found the woman in the closet, unconscious and clutching a Bible with burned hands. Up and over her shoulder. Mai did the same thing five more times, the smoke overwhelming her a little more with each rescue, the fire both weakening and strengthening her as she made her way through the building, grabbing limp bodies, resisting bodies, alive bodies. Like an assembly line, one after the other. She left the dead ones to their rest.

"Mercy! Mercy!"

"My son! You said you'd save my son!" The woman still struggled in the arms of her neighbors, her thin nightgown dark with smoke and falling off her narrow shoulders. Her teeth were sharp and fierce in her face, stripped down to the basic drive of a mother wanting to protect her child. It wasn't something Mai was familiar with, but she'd seen it in documentaries.

A blush of shame rushed through her. Up and up, perched at the top, the boy huddled frozen in terror. All he had to do was jump, but it was not going to happen. He was too scared.

Shit. She'd gotten distracted. Firefighters were coming. But they wouldn't get to the boy in time.

"Jump!" the woman screamed to her son. "Ty! Please, just jump!"

More people gathered below the window despite the flames spouting from the top of the building, encouraging him to jump with the outstretched protection of their arms. Not the most brilliant idea.

Mai cursed again, then ran back into the building.

Coughing.

Choking.

Her lungs were already tight and scorched from pulling in too little oxygen. Her senses swam. It was too late. She knew it when she reached through the fire, clambering up the superheated bricks that lit up the palms of her bare hands with pain. She'd screwed up and left the boy waiting too long.

His room door was cinders now. The flames flew across the carpet of his bedroom, devouring everything it could. Bedsheets. Toys. Posters of cars. His flesh teased the fire. It, too, would easily burn. All of him would burn.

The window felt even farther than before, its ledge practically glowing with heat. How could the boy sit in a heat so intense? When she finally got to him, she knew how. He was a statue of flesh transformed by terror into a panting but otherwise frozen thing.

"It's okay." She said the words even though she barely believed them. She wrapped the boy's body with her own and jumped, a quick breath up and out the window just as a fireball exploded in the room and blasted them out into the cool air.

Mai clutched the boy, whimpering now, as they flew through the air. She heard a rising tide of gasps below and controlled her own exhalation, used the momentum of the blast, and turned them in the air, keeping as much of her own body as possible wrapped around him. Something hard slammed into her back, drove the breath from her lungs. The side of the nearby building. She held on to enough presence of mind to roll down and cushion their fall with her body, leaving the boy untouched.

Mai felt rather than heard the people flooding toward them in concern. She stood, cursing her own stupidity, and lifted the boy, barely any weight at all, as she looked through the crush of people for his mother.

"Thank God!" The woman screamed her son's name and reached for him, the tendons of her neck etched in stark relief. Her nails scraped Mai's hands as she clutched her son.

Mai stood still long enough to make sure the woman easily bore the burden of the boy, then she spun away, ignoring the cries of the crowd shouting her name to finally pay attention to her body's aches and wounds. One alley, then two. Her arms stretched and burned as she reached up to lever herself higher and higher. By the time she reached a tenth-story rooftop, she felt better. The boy was alive. Traumatized, but she'd blame that on the fire instead of her own carelessness.

Before long, she was back where she started. A rooftop downtown.

In the aftermath of the fire, her breath heaved and her muscles were loose and warm. Pleasure sang through her veins. This was what she had needed. This combination of usefulness and danger. Accelerated heartbeat and eased fears.

Going home to her own bed would be another pleasure. But only after she shared a different kind of pleasure with the stranger downstairs. She imagined waking to the softness of the woman's body, a moaning greeting, and then an explosive climax in the heat of her lover's embrace. A perfect bookend to the night.

Mai quickly descended to the woman's room. As quietly as she could, she showered the stink of adrenaline and smoke from her skin and slipped between the sheets, curling the length of her body around the resting woman. Sleep came as easily as the next breath.

CHAPTER 2

"AND THAT'S ALL THERE IS to know about incest in royal European families, ladies and everyone else. See you next week." Mai took off the glasses she didn't need—the equivalent of closing her instructor's copy of the textbook—and waved her students away with them.

The group of mostly sophomores quickly gathered their books and rushed toward the door, obviously glad for the Friday evening seminar to be over. Two or three stragglers hung back, talking with each other, and a few more made a beeline for Mai's desk, naked worship and hope in their faces.

She kept her expression professional yet casual, not filled with the seductive invitation a few of her colleagues regularly practiced on the impressionable group of students.

"Can I come see you during your office hours, Professor Redstone?" Beatrice Aarondale, one of her more intelligent students and coincidentally one of Mai's ardent pursuers, cocked her hip and gave her a honeyed smile. Blue lipstick and smoky eye makeup highlighted her already-pretty face. A white off-the-shoulder dress hugged her thick breasts and hips. "There are a few points from the class I'm not clear on."

Mai resisted the urge to roll her eyes. "Of course. Check for the availability of office hours with my TA." She tipped her chin toward Carol, who sat in the back of the room, already looking over the papers she'd collected from the students at the beginning of class.

"Okay, thanks." But Beatrice still stood there, aggressively sexy, until one of her friends nudged her in the back and fought his way in front of her to hand Mai a book he'd borrowed the previous class.

Mai accepted the book with a smile and slid it into her slim leather briefcase. As she looked up from putting the book away, a figure passing the open door of her classroom caught her eye. Her stomach dipped.

Xóchitl Bentley. A suitably complex name for the seemingly complex woman who'd come to the campus a semester before from one of Atlanta's biggest and best private universities. Mai had heard through the grapevine that she spent the first class of each semester teaching her students how to say her name.

Xóchitl. *Show cheel.*

The day Mai stumbled into Xóchitl Bentley, she'd literally lost her breath, left quietly panting by the fist of desire in her belly that had been both powerful and unexpected.

In the hallway outside Mai's classroom, the woman swept through the wave of students like they weren't even there, graceful and cool like an iceberg sitting in winter waters and careless of the ships or high waves or anything else nearby. Mai grew weak just at the sight of her.

Tonight, Xóchitl wore a dress—loose-fitting cotton in all white, but with an incongruous Guatemalan print satchel over her shoulder. On her feet, bright yellow high heels tapped an insistent rhythm that echoed in the pit of Mai's stomach.

Xóchitl was graceful, delicate, and gorgeous. And she wasn't the least bit interested in Mai.

Once her own interest was established and nothing overtly reciprocal came from Xóchitl, Mai thought the other professor wasn't into women. But an illicit night on Facebook had yielded evidence to the contrary. The very next moment, Mai had thoughts of trickery, sudden and innate, of shifting some small thing about herself, her face, her figure, downplaying the femininity of her walk to change and become something more like the AG, or butch, women she'd seen on Xóchitl's arm online. This was something she could easily accomplish as a Meta human, a minor bit of manipulation compared to what she'd seen others do.

But the thought both disgusted and terrified Mai. She didn't want to be like most of the Metas she knew, ruthlessly exploitive and remorseless. So she avoided Xóchitl from that day on. It didn't stop her from looking, though.

Mai blinked away from the tempting vision in the hallway when someone touched her arm, then abruptly let go.

"Your skin is so warm!" Beatrice looked down at her own hand as if she expected it to be burned. "Do you have a fever or something?"

Mai was still distracted by Xóchitl. That was the only reason she slipped and said, "I'm just a little hot-blooded, that's all."

"I bet."

She pursed her lips, annoyed at herself for giving shameless Beatrice such an obvious opening. She met her student's gaze with a slight reprimanding shake of her head. "If there isn't anything else, I'll see you in my office."

Before Beatrice could say a word either way, Mai's phone chirped, a burst of sound only she could hear.

"Excuse me," she said to the small group of students and swept up her briefcase while deftly fishing the cell phone, her car keys, and a protein bar from her desk drawer. "I'll see you all next time. If you need anything before then, call my office or send an e-mail."

She arranged her belongings in various pockets of the briefcase, her keys jingling in her hand as she headed out of the building toward the parking lot, already suspecting what the person on the other end of the phone line had to say. The call came at a good time, though. She needed the distraction. "Yes?" she said into the phone.

"Can you drop by the station on Monday?" A familiar voice asked the question in lieu of a hello.

"Yes."

"Six in the evening?"

"Yes."

"Good."

Stepping out into the warm embrace of the September evening, she put away the phone, heels like silenced gunshots against the still sun-heated concrete of the parking deck. Her car beeped when she disarmed the alarm, and the relief of being away from so many eyes and in a private space made her sigh with quiet pleasure. She dropped her bag in the passenger seat.

"You'd have much more fun if you worked at your mother's company."

It was only an intense act of will that prevented her from lashing out to protect herself. Mai tightened her fist around the car key. She felt more than heard the minute sigh of her leather stilettos as her toes flexed and spread wide, her body readying itself to spring into action. Her fighting instinct had never learned to relax around family.

"What do you want, Ethan?"

Her cousin sat in her back seat, smug in his Tom Ford three-piece suit and shark's grin. "You, as always."

He sat in her car, looking for all the world like he belonged there. A muscle throbbed in Mai's jaw as she waited for him to get to the point of his visit.

"Nice car," he said, grinding down her patience even more. He shifted obscenely behind her, hands caressing the leather seat on either side of his sprawled thighs.

Just because her mother gave him the power to do whatever he wanted in pursuit of her orders, he felt free to be an asshole, which included flirting with Mai when he knew damn well she didn't date men. He made no secret that he thought he would one day be the permanent exception to Mai's "no men allowed" rule. But despite how things stood between Mai and her powerful mother, Mandaia Redstone would never approve a marriage between Mai and Ethan.

So she waited him out while he felt up the napa leather of her well-loved Mercedes. Mai started the car and cued up Nicki Minaj on the Bluetooth connection to her phone. When "Anaconda" began to play, her cousin started talking, but Mai didn't turn down the music. Neither of them needed silence to hear each other.

"Your mother wants me to remind you about the Conclave of Families tomorrow afternoon."

Mai rolled her eyes. As if she could forget. On every single day last week, her mother had made a point of texting her various details of the Conclave—what time it started, where she would sit when the official announcements were made, what to wear.

Ever since Mai had neglected to go to the last Conclave, which was nothing more than a glorified birthday party for a child too spoiled to appreciate the small island her cash-rich but power-poor family had bought for her, Mandaia's messages to her daughter had been rife with even more disappointment than usual. Mai liked to pretend that it didn't matter.

"Okay," Mai said with a dismissive glance at her cousin. "You've reminded me. Now go."

His face flashed spite in her rearview mirror, his shark teeth on full display. "Formal dress," he hissed at her. "Something showing off that hot body of yours."

Ethan gave the nut-brown leather another suggestive caress as he stared past the driver's seat at her body. It was as if he were seeing through to her naked skin. Mai wouldn't put it past him to do just that.

Annoyed, she put the car in gear and drove off. Caught off guard, her cousin abruptly melted through the leather upholstery, his body going completely transparent before slipping through the leather, then out of her car. She didn't need to look back to see him standing on the moonlit parking deck, hands in the pockets of his gray suit, his figure solid once more.

"See that you're there. You don't want to disappoint her." A pocket of sound burst near her ear, the last remnant of his unwanted visit.

She turned up the stereo and rolled down all the windows. But the reminder of his presence still lingered like a bad stench.

CHAPTER 3

MAI NEVER FELT LIKE SHE belonged in her family. Well, maybe not quite never, but close enough. The last time she'd felt as if she belonged, she was a naïve twelve-year-old. Twenty years of betrayal and pain separated that child from who she was now.

She drew in a deep and steadying breath and slowly released it.

With her tiny purse tucked under her arm, she stood at the top of the main staircase of her mother's Alpharetta mansion, watching the annual Conclave from a distance. A meeting of all the Families in North America to discuss pertinent Meta business, the Conclave was nearly over. Mai had planned it that way.

This was the last place she wanted to be. Her stomach twisted with discomfort, and she could barely get her legs to move forward. Other than to attend official gatherings, she hadn't been in her family home since she moved out nearly seventeen years before for boarding school. It was seventeen years of peace she'd desperately claimed for herself after the horror of living in a house where she couldn't be safe.

Okay. Enough. Mai shook herself and took a deliberate step forward. She couldn't stand there stewing in her resentment all afternoon. *Shit or get off the pot.* But she couldn't push herself to go any further.

A hand curled around the dark wooden railing, while the other tightened into a fist in her pocket. She drew in another deep breath, this one too deep, and almost choked on the sickly sweet scent of tropical flowers that hung thick and cloudlike throughout the entire mansion. Her spine stiffened.

In defiance of what her mother expected, Mai wore slacks. Slim-fitting tuxedo pants the color of old blood, a white blouse sheer enough to show off the shape of her braless breasts underneath, and the unapologetic opacity of her nipples that wilted in the warm room. She wore the brief outfit like armor, a visual reminder to everyone that she knew she didn't fit in among them and would never try.

Below the landing where she stood, two sweeping parallel staircases led down to the main ballroom where over five dozen people gathered, members of the sixteen Meta Families living in the North American territory. Above them, the ceiling soared two stories high, terminating in a wide and round stained glass feature that poured brilliant sunlight down on everyone gathered for the biannual event.

Their combined voices rose and fell through the massive room, weaving with the music from the string quartet tucked away on the smaller of two stages in the ballroom.

Everyone looked beautiful. Powerful. Even the members of the Families with little Meta power exuded influence because of the financial sway they held in the human world. Energy in the room rolled, warm and electric, over Mai's skin like an unwanted caress, stirring up her self-protective instincts.

She didn't belong among these Metas. But she didn't fully belong in the human world either. The only time she felt truly like herself was when she dressed in the skin of her own choosing and blended into the night on rooftops and alleys all over the city. *That* felt right.

With her family, she just felt like prey.

Below her, the high afternoon Conclave continued on, despite her lack of direct involvement, and Mai was glad for it. She knew, though, that she couldn't stay above it for long. Just then, a gong sounded, deep and overly dramatic, a signal for everyone to stop what they were doing and move toward the raised dais in front of the massive ballroom.

"So you actually decided to grace us with your presence today."

Mai turned to look over her shoulder, keeping her hand on the balustrade for balance. A very distant cousin, Caressa, came up slowly behind her. Even Caressa's approach, friend though she was, was a cautious one, as if approaching some rabid and untamed animal. Everyone knew that although Mai was nearly powerless, she was vicious when cornered and wore her body like a naked blade. This reputation was her only defense among other Metas, and she was proud of it.

"Mother just about threatened me, so I couldn't say no this time." Caressa knew Mandaia well enough to know Mai wasn't joking.

Caressa, being only a low-level empath, had as little power as Mai. But Caressa had taken the path recommended by her own mother and gone into politics, easily charming every human she met and parlaying that into a seat in the Senate. One of the youngest senators in the country at the age of forty, she was well on her way to more and better. It was a strategic position to be in if the future clash between humans and Metas that her brother and his radical friends were always talking about ever became a reality.

"Threats must look good on you, then." Caressa leveled a flirtatious look at Mai, who was used to this sort of behavior from her. She seemed to think Mai wanted this sort of thing.

That was absolutely *not* what Mai was projecting. Here of all places, she held her emotions tightly locked in a cage. But Caressa was ridiculously beautiful and thought everyone wanted to fuck her.

She teased Mai again with a dip of her emerald eyes, scanning her from Mai's high crown of hair to the black stilettos that were like daggers on her feet. "Come down with me and stop lurking up here like a ghoul." She slipped her arm through Mai's without waiting for agreement and tugged her down the steps.

The ballroom was large, just one of the many showplaces in the massive house. Even among their powerful and mostly rich race of Meta humans, Mandaia Redstone was extremely wealthy. Instead of going into politics like most Metas, she'd opted to go into media and business. She had an extremely successful talk show for nearly thirty years before she gave it all up to become a business mogul and focus full-time on amassing even more money and working behind the scenes to pull the strings of America's conscience and its political institutions. Mandaia Redstone was very good at pulling strings.

This house of hers was one few humans knew about. According to paperwork available to any enterprising hacker or diligent googler, Mandaia lived on a twenty-acre ranch somewhere in California and owned over a dozen homes in other parts of the world. But this mansion was her primary home where she, as matriarch of the Redstone Family, lived, hosted Conclaves, and showed fledgling Metas what to aspire to. Her benevolent mask was a beautiful and believable one. Mai sometimes wished she'd never seen what was behind it.

The gong sounded again, a thirty-second warning.

"You really waited until the last minute to get here, didn't you?" Caressa tilted her head down at Mai, who was a full three inches shorter.

They flowed down the stairs and into the crowd with the rest of the stragglers.

"You say it often enough yourself," Mai said. "Why waste valuable time on the things you don't want to do?"

She wasn't telling Caressa anything new. Just about everyone knew how much Mai hated these events, the pomposity of it all. The unnecessary expense of the parties. The hypocrisy at the idea of family, when any of them were willing to sacrifice their young for... anything.

As she approached the gathered crowd, Mai felt her mother's gaze on her and turned to meet it—amber eyes the same shade as hers, loosened curls tumbling around her silk-clad shoulders, and a face so beautiful it seemed unreal. It *was* unreal. Mai blinked and looked away.

On the dais behind her mother like a royal retinue sat members of Mai's immediate family: her younger sister, Abi, who could influence living and dying things; their father, Quinn, whose power was invulnerability to everything except old age and his wife's machinations; and Mai's younger brother, Cayman, who could break anything on earth with his mind alone.

From behind their mother's back, her sister fluttered long fingers at Mai in greeting, risking a small smile. Mai wondered if their mother had noticed. Mai's own smile died before it could be born when she noticed Ethan had taken her place on the dais. He was a mid-level teleporter, avid sycophant, and local mobster with growing influence on the East Coast. Beside him was his father—and Mai's uncle—Stephen, a level-ten telekinetic. She quickly skimmed her gaze over her uncle, not wanting to have him in her sight any longer than necessary.

Looking at them reminded Mai again how much of an anomaly she was among her Power-rich family. She was only a chameleon, able to change surface parts of herself to alter her appearance. Her hearing, sight, and speed were superhuman. But that was ordinary among Metas.

When she was a child, her mother had thought she could be more and tried to force that perceived potential into becoming a reality. That force had yielded nothing but Mai's fear and Mandaia's disappointment. Mai remained as she was.

It was that powerlessness which had left Mai vulnerable as a child.

Even with her Redstone Family weakness, Mai was still more powerful than many members of the other Families who'd bred out their Meta power over the centuries by having children with humans. Only in the last twenty years had Metas begun to pay attention to what Mandaia Redstone had been saying all along, that the Families needed to create fertile marriages between Metas and secure power in the blood. It helped that the Redstones were unique, in that all their members had some sort of power.

Which was why Mandaia Redstone was the matriarch and current head of all Families in North America.

Her mother began speaking from the stage. "Greetings and continued prosperity for doing me the honor of attending this most humble event."

Caressa tried to tug her toward the stage, but Mai dug in her heels. She was close enough. Very gently, she unwound her arm from her cousin's and put a few inches of distance between them, ignoring Caressa's slightly hurt look. Her skin was tingling with the need to morph into something that would protect her from the danger she sensed on the stage. But there was no mask she could put on, no new chin, no hunched back, no artificially heightened frame that would protect her from what she knew her mother was capable of.

Still, Mai straightened her spine and widened her stance, hands in her pockets, where she felt the small, rectangular, card-sized case where she carried her ID, a few folded bills, and the single key to her car. Her apartment was electronically locked with her fingerprint and a scrambled code, so she didn't need to carry those keys.

"Today, we have come together to announce and celebrate the engagement of Audrina Page and Rafael Hernandez," her mother continued.

As she spoke, two people approached her from opposite sides of the stage—a pretty teenager and a man who looked about Mai's age. Despite her makeup, it was obvious the girl was young, maybe sixteen years old, and that was being generous. She looked Instagram-ready in her floor-length gilded gown that brought out the gold in her own skin. Her hair was a tall and impressive wave of brown silk studded with diamond pins.

Mai wouldn't have been surprised to see a photo of the girl on social media later, pouting toward the audience with her skillfully applied makeup and diamond nose ring. She looked proud to have the Hernandez Family claim on her. But her too-wide eyes and flickering smile betrayed that she wasn't quite sure what she was doing. She was so damn young.

Mai couldn't imagine the amount of money the Hernandez Family had pledged for Mandaia to agree to this.

"Audrina." Mandaia held out her hand, and the girl stepped forward, the skirts of her gold gown brushing the floor and swirling around her long legs. Audrina put her right hand in Mandaia's, and a flare of electricity burned through the room. For the first time, the girl looked frightened. But she kept her hand in Mandaia's even though the contact with her mother's tremendous power must have hurt. "Rafael." Her mother called over the fiancé-to-be.

Rafael Hernandez stepped forward, looking more confident and capable, as befitting a man at least ten years older than Audrina. He put his hand in Mandaia's left palm, and electricity licked through the room again. On the dais, Rafael flinched but kept his hand where it needed to be, probably not wanting to be outdone by his child-fiancée.

"Unless any Family has some reason why this arrangement should not come to pass…" And Mandaia paused in the traditional manner, something obviously taken from human ceremonies, waiting to see if there were any objections. When all that came was silence, she continued. "Audrina Page and Rafael Hernandez are hereby pledged to each other. The wedding will occur in three years' time, when Audrina comes of age."

Mandaia brought up her open palms, burdened with the hands of the two people who had pledged to join their lives together. The room sparked with the smell of ozone and a flash of blue light as the rings on the pinky fingers of the couple caught both the light and the power in the room.

"Long life and power to you." The entire ballroom rumbled with the combined voices of the hundreds of Metas gathered as they said the traditional words.

Electric heat raced through the air, heating Mai's skin and everyone else's, a source of comfort and a connection to a distant power her mother always speculated was tied into the origin of all Metas. Mai's skin tingled and flushed. As the closest female relative to her mother and the one who in theory would inherit her position should Mandaia see fit to leave the earth to less deserving mortals, she felt an echo of the power surge that her mother experienced during the pledge.

The rising tide of applause pulled her attention from her mother and to the rest of the gathered crowd. Beside her, Caressa was clapping along with the rest of them to ceremonially serenade the couple's walk down the stairs and into the crowd. Mai's hands stayed at her sides.

Despite the distance between them, she caught her mother's eyes. The darkly golden gaze held Mai's with a ferocity she'd grown used to over the years but had never learned to properly protect herself from. Mandaia was pissed Mai had waited so long to arrive at the ceremony.

Tough shit.

She broke eye contact with her mother and turned from the dais, stepping away from Caressa at the same time with the excuse of reaching for a glass of champagne from a nearby waiter. She didn't want the alcohol, but the glass felt cool in her palm. Grounding. She sipped the champagne, her nose twitching from the bubbles.

At the edge of her awareness, she noticed her uncle drift away from the rest of the family and migrate into the crowd. In his bespoke iron-gray suit and smile meant to charm, he should have been reeling men and women alike into his orbit; after all, he was attractive enough, in the way that everyone in Mai's family was. But people only came close enough to him to be polite, perhaps even to pretend to like him, their distaste apparent in the stiff way they held their bodies, in the way they didn't look at him for too long.

Mai breathed out her own dislike, trying but failing to wrench her gaze from her uncle and to will away the sudden tightness in her chest the sight of him caused. He turned, and Mai froze in the snare of his smile, ice coating her spine.

A shoulder bumped into hers from behind, jostling the champagne glass in her hands and threatening to push her off the stilts of her shoes. She flinched. Only her quick reflexes saved her from drenching her shirt with the wine or stumbling into someone standing nearby. Mai had never been more grateful for rudeness in her life.

"Cayman."

Her brother grinned at her, showing his perfect teeth. His square-jawed good looks and friendly smile were identical to their father's. The only thing he'd inherited from Mandaia were her piercing wolf eyes. That was enough to make Mai glance away from him for a moment. She refused to look where she'd just seen her uncle.

"Mandaia-Pili." His grin widened as he called her by her full name. *Mandaia the Second.* She winced as if the name hurt. "Nice outfit," he said, flicking a gaze over her sheer blouse and tuxedo pants. "I bet Mother loves it."

"Good thing I didn't wear it for her."

"Or did you?" Cayman amped up his grin. "Whatever the end goal, you definitely got her attention." He slid his hands into the pockets of his tuxedo slacks and tossed a casual glance around them. Although he would never inherit what their mother had—Families relied on female heirs—he took in the massive ballroom, with its endless crowd of beautiful people and the gold, silver, and marble fixtures, as if he owned it and Mai didn't.

Thanks to years of practice, she didn't react. She deliberately trailed her eyes away from her brother to the sight of Caressa making her way through the thick crowd of Metas and their spouses, smiling and making small talk while heading for Mandaia, the real object of her attention. Caressa had always been ambitious in a way that Mai was not, stroking opportunities until she felt the perfect moment to strike. She was a brilliant strategist, something Mandaia had always admired. And respected.

In their world, it was eat or be eaten, take or be taken, and Caressa had balanced her life perfectly on the knife's edge of taking care of herself and making sure no one else took her. Her politics were brilliant, and even Mai, who hated the necessary Family machinations with every bone in her body, had to admire her.

Mai's own solution to survival was to stay away from the family and other Metas as much as she was able. It didn't always quite work out.

Beside her, Cayman plucked his ringing phone from the inside pocket of his jacket and spoke softly into it for a few seconds before putting it away. He looked more intentionally around the room then. After apparently not finding what he was looking for, he gave a faint shrug. He grabbed his phone again and fired off a quick text in a flurry of thumbs.

"Mother was looking for you earlier." He tucked his phone back into his pocket and turned back to Mai.

"She always knows where to find me."

Her brother nodded. "True enough." Then he gave up his pose of nonchalance and draped himself over the railing, elbows propped up on the swirled marble, grinning like the unpretentious, carefree boy he used to be before…everything happened.

Something down below made his smile turn into a laugh, and he turned to Mai as if he was going to share the joke, then seemed to remember what they'd become to each other. Nearly enemies. His mouth thinned, and he looked back down at the moving crowd. "The only person she can't find right now is Uncle Stephen. She's calling for him with no luck."

"I'm sure he's taking care of his own business. He'll come back later to give her a perfectly acceptable excuse for his absence."

Mai didn't care where Stephen Redstone had disappeared to. Her uncle was a state senator, hunting enthusiast, and raging asshole. He was also the favorite of her mother's three siblings. This wasn't his first sudden disappearance from an event her mother thought was important, and it wouldn't be the last.

"That guy is a dick." Cayman sounded jealous. He was nowhere near the favored anything. The only advantage he had in the family, aside from his Meta power, was that he wasn't Mai. "He could've at least waited until this whole bullshit was over before skipping out. Mandaia is pissed."

"I am no such thing."

Mai briefly closed her eyes and relaxed her hand around the champagne glass until she felt that it would simply fall from her hand and shatter on the floor. Her mother touched a palm to the center of Mai's back, a warm and heavy weight.

Anyone watching would probably think it was a touch of affection. But Mai felt the rake of her mother's Power checking on her state of mind and making sure she functioned as she always had. A quick look that bypassed Mai's deeper thoughts was the only courtesy her mother gave her. Mai clenched her teeth and bore the assault in silence.

"I'm happy you were able to find your way here despite your prior obligations, Mai." She took her hand away, allowing Mai a quiet breath of relief.

"I told you I would come, Mother." She took a healthy sip of her champagne, although she wished it were whiskey instead.

"You just didn't say what time you would come." Her mother clicked her teeth around the last word. "I know. Always the trickster, Mandaia-Pili."

On unsteady legs, Mai moved away from her mother. One step and then two. "You don't want me around any more than I want to be here, Mother. I was doing us both a favor by showing up as late as I did." Mandaia released a harsh breath, and Mai frowned when she realized it was a habit she'd also picked up over the years. Her annoyance at it made her feel foolish. "I thought Stephen would occupy your attentions, and you'd forget all about your defect daughter."

Her mother hissed and struck, fast as a cobra, fingers digging into Mai's elbow. "That's unnecessary, Mai."

Mai nodded and pulled her elbow away despite the added pain of scraping her skin against her mother's sharp fingernails. "This is my cue to leave, I think." She stepped back another foot. "Give Father and Abi my regards. I'll see everyone at the next family dinner." She said the last words loud enough for anyone listening to hear. Mai had no intention of eating with her family ever again.

Although Mandaia could have done any number of things to keep Mai at her side, she let her go, and Mai left the ballroom with her typical slow and swaying walk. Her heart thundered like the hooves of wild horses.

CHAPTER 4

AT HOME, MAI COULDN'T GET her clothes off fast enough. Her blouse stank of her mother's mansion, of the jasmine and other hothouse flowers that hung like funeral wreaths everywhere. She threw her clothes into the washer, dry cleaning tags be damned, and took a long and hot shower to scrub all traces of the gathering from her skin.

But the shower didn't scrub the afternoon's events from her mind. So she buried herself in the work of grading papers and refining the syllabus for the new Caribbean literature class she planned for next semester. Soon enough, she fell into the rhythm of the tasks she loved, working late into the night and past her bedtime. Only when her eyes started to droop at 2:00 a.m. did she give up and get ready for bed. Thoughts of her students lulled her easily into sleep.

Mai dreams of drowning. Terror soaked and panting, she struggles under the sheet, aware she is dreaming but unable to wake up. Her pulse tries to hammer its way from under her skin. Her heartbeat is deafening. It takes a forever of incomplete breaths, but she does eventually manage to open her eyes. She gulps greedily at the air, still lost in the dream but closer to her own reality, staring hot-eyed at the bare, white ceiling of her bedroom. Her chest vibrates with fright while the memory of high water ripples behind her eyelids. Even semiawake from the dreams she's had too often since she was a child, she still feels the phantom sensation of someone trapping her wrists above her head, water pressing against her nose, and a gentle hand holding her beneath the liquid surge.

"Mama," she whimpers in the prison of her sweat-damp sheets and feels shame for it.

There was no one to save her then, and no one to save her now.

Mai opens her mouth to scream.

The jarring clang of her phone's private ringtone yanked her fully out of the dream. Mai swallowed the aborted cry. Chest still heaving, she rolled over in the twisted sheets, grateful for her easy breaths, and reached for her iPhone on the bedside table.

"Yes?"

"Can you come now?"

She squinted at the time. It was barely four o'clock in the morning. "I thought you wanted to see me Monday."

"That's irrelevant now. Something else came up." Although the voice on the other end of the line was smooth and unhurried, there was no mistaking the sense of urgency.

"Alright. Give me forty-five minutes."

"Thirty would be better."

After brushing her teeth and changing into Mercy's skin, Mai took to the rooftops and made it to the Midtown building in twenty minutes. It was an old structure that used to be a human police station until Metas bought it and made it their own.

She dropped down from the roof, easily making the six-story jump to land on quiet feet in the narrow alley between two Meta-owned buildings. At this time of morning, Atlanta was mostly quiet, with only the occasional car passing on the street, the moon a high and bright crescent, and clouds drifting across the still-dark sky. The early fall breeze brushed over her mostly naked skin.

When she stepped into the building, it was like a regular workday. Or in this case, early morning. High-wattage fluorescents spotlighted the dozen or so desks arranged in two neat rows in the large main room. At these desks were Metas all dressed in black—some seated, others standing. At the end of the short double rows of desks stood a door of frosted glass—a typical-looking if small police station staffed by Metas charged with investigating crimes by and against their own.

Already used to her presence, few paid her any attention as she made her way toward the closed door. She knocked once before letting herself in.

The office was large, more typical of a conference room with its centrally placed table, an equally long whiteboard spread across the front wall, and a set of windows with a one-way view of the tree-lined parking lot. Three enforcers stood at the back of the massive office. They were all dressed in black—long-sleeved shirts tucked into soft-looking denim and knee-high boots. Their red and yellow starburst insignias blazed on each shirt's right breast.

With arms crossed, the enforcers scowled at an electronic projection lit up in thin, blue light. Although none of them were obviously armed, they all exuded an air of deadly efficiency and purpose. Anyone, human or Meta, would be a fool to take them on, despite their faces, which even under the universally unflattering florescent lights were all grimly attractive—the apex of Meta beauty and power.

"Sorry to drag you out of bed," Denali, the region commander, said, although he didn't look sorry, "but we have a situation."

Tall and with severe features that belied him being the most approachable of his colleagues, Denali gestured for Mai to come close. He didn't turn from the projection casting eerie blue shadows over his face and those of the two others in the room, Nuala and Ty.

"There's been a murder, by a Meta." Nuala, nearly as tall as the commander and with sleepy eyes that hid her laserlike attention to every detail, turned to Mai. "We found the body less than an hour ago."

Mai shuddered. *What Meta would dare?*

Punishable crime was relatively low in their society. Every one of them knew that to attract the attention of the enforcers was to essentially surrender everything. Their power. Their money. Their lives. The enforcers always found who they were looking for, and there were no enforcer prisons.

"Who's this victim?" she asked.

The name Denali said made Mai's ears ring. "Excuse me?" She must have heard wrong. There was no way he just said—

He repeated the name, but it wasn't any easier to process the second time. Mai's muscles twitched with the sudden need to put her body in motion, to leap across the room and get in Denali's face, and demand he say those words one more time. She crossed her arms over her chest but otherwise stayed still.

That doesn't...

Mai cut off her train of thought and forced all her disbelief to the back of her mind. "What happened?" She finally paced to the window, unable to bear the ticking in her muscles much longer.

"The Absolution Killer." Ty spoke up for the first time, his voice a hoarse menace, a permanent reminder of a Meta criminal who'd tried to crush his throat.

As always, his broken voice made Mai want to touch her own neck in a useless gesture of self-protection. Instead, she drew in a slow breath and focused on the view outside the window.

Absolution. That...makes sense.

A killer who'd never been caught but always left clues about who they were killing, and why. Now that their latest victim was a powerful Meta, it only made sense to assume Absolution was a Meta too. A strong one.

The trees across the parking lot rustled from the touch of a passing breeze, the sound like a flurry of whispers reaching out to Mai from the past. A faint, rattling noise distracted her stare out the window. Her fingers were trembling. Knocking against the windowpane. She clenched her hands tight and walked past the enforcers to look at the files spread out on the conference table.

She touched one of the older ones, darkened and curled at the edges from repeated handling: Twenty-eight men and nine women killed over the last six years, found in very public spaces, their bodies maimed and facial features nearly unrecognizable from prolonged torture. And there had always been a note stuffed into their mouths after death.

I CONFESS, the notes said. All of them were in the victims' own shaky handwriting.

The human police named the killer "Absolution" because of these notes, signs of the killer forcing these murdered men and women to acknowledge some crime they'd committed and maybe even seek pardon for them.

By the nature of the torture—fingers smashed, genitals mutilated, orifices ruthlessly penetrated by foreign objects before death—the murders seemed motivated by revenge for sexual wrongs. During the five years Mai had been working with enforcers, the Absolution Killer had taken three victims in Atlanta alone. Unlike human law enforcement, not once had the Tribunal of Enforcers officially taken notice of the killer, who'd seemed to target mostly humans and a few low-power Metas. These Meta victims had lived completely as human and had been assumed to be the result of human/Meta mixing. Since the murders technically weren't committed against Metas, or at least not within their walled-off society, the enforcers had largely ignored Absolution's career. Instead, they had been amused by what they saw as an efficient human killer taking out the trash in his own community. But now...

"What can I do here that you can't?" Mai asked.

Nuala made a sound that wasn't a laugh. "You know the answer to that question."

Unfortunately, Mai did. As Mandaia-Pili Redstone, she had crucial access to this victim's family that the enforcers did not. If she was reading the situation right, they also expected her to use that access to investigate every aspect of his life, find out what he'd done to attract Absolution's interest, and hopefully find a trail leading to the killer. She skimmed through the files on the table briefly looked at the electronic display she suddenly realized showed the locations of all known Absolution kills.

"Okay," Mai said. "I'll do my best."

Denali drifted to her side, close enough to touch her. But he didn't. "You can start by going downstairs with Nuala to the morgue and taking a look at what we have to work with," he said. "The other

Absolution kills were easy enough for a human. This one…" His shoulder brushed Mai's, a wordless offer of apology after what he had just asked her to do. "A Meta clearly did this, and we're going to catch them."

Mai drew in another long and silent breath, preparing to refuse. The photographs should be enough to lead her where she needed to go. But then she thought of another audience she was sure to have and its particular set of questions.

"I'm ready whenever you are," she said and swallowed the last of her unease.

Death had never disturbed her. It came to everyone eventually. It would come for her soon enough. While she hadn't managed to make total peace with it, it was not something she flinched from. And she would not start now, even when it was her uncle on the steel slab.

CHAPTER 5

When Mai saw Stephen Redstone's face, her heart kicked hard in her chest. He had died screaming. No amount of sanitized lighting could hide that.

"We waited until you came to start." The Meta medical examiner grumbled this at Mai as she settled within sight of her uncle's body. She swiped eucalyptus gel under her nose to dull the smell in the room, then crossed her arms tight over her chest. The ME picked up his instruments and began. He delicately plucked away pieces of the body, unfolding the story as clearly as if Mai had been there to see every moment of his torture.

Stephen Redstone had been taken by someone he'd thought was harmless. Neither of his hands had any defensive wounds. His belly had been full of a good meal before the torture began—Indian spiced tea, cardamom cookies, a yogurt-rich dinner wreathed in spinach and supplemented with piece after piece of butter-slathered naan bread. He had been aroused at some point during the evening—Mai assumed it was evening since seductions of this sort usually happened under the cover of dark. Her uncle had always preferred the dark.

He must have tried to bribe his way out of the situation. In addition to the piece of paper in his mouth with the scrawled *I CONFESS* were the torn halves of three different hundred-dollar bills. They were stuffed halfway down his throat. He must have choked on them as he screamed for his life, enraged that someone had gotten enough of a drop on him to... And that was where the ME's details became vague, or at least began to seem like bald-faced guesses. Mai knew her uncle. He was arrogant about his physical near invulnerability, but that didn't mean he never took precautions, just in case.

He'd been tied up. Rough pieces of something abrasive and ropelike had secured him without being too tight. But after a while, he'd struggled against them, tearing at his skin and rubbing it raw. Thick, clotting blood and stripped flesh around both wrists and ankles testified to that.

After he realized there was no point to his struggles or bribes or threats, that was when Absolution *really* got to work, slashing nearly every surface area of skin with what could have been a scalpel. Stephen's penis had been severed and stuffed into his rectum with what could have been a Coke bottle or a butt plug. Mai was laying odds on the Coke bottle. She wouldn't put it past this killer to know how much her uncle enjoyed his Coca-Cola. Right up until the very end, apparently. Or maybe not exactly "enjoyed."

But how had Absolution caught him? Mai snorted. *With his dick, most likely.*

"You agree it was another Meta who did this?" Nuala asked her once the ME was done performing his macabre parlor tricks and dismissed them.

Stephen Redstone's telekinetic ability was the strongest Mai had ever known. Even with his body weakened, he should have been able to wrap his mind around any object in the room and at the very least, bludgeon his captor to death. But he hadn't.

"Yes." Mai walked out of the room with Nuala at her heels.

She pulled the surgical mask from her face and used it to wipe the now-warm eucalyptus gel from under her nose. Briefly, she squeezed her eyes shut. The images of her uncle's empty body felt permanently seared behind her eyelids. A painful lump rolled at the base of her throat. She swallowed and swallowed but couldn't get rid of it.

Standing in the starkly lit hallway, Mai drew in even breaths, hoping Nuala wouldn't notice. It was hard enough for her to ignore the fine shudders in her own limbs, the coldness settling into her core. The flimsy surgical mask fluttered with each tremor of her hand.

"This Absolution Killer, this Meta, must be punished." Nuala stood a little straighter as she aimed the words at Mai, her expression implacable, as if Mai herself stood between her and her intended prey.

"But only now that they've killed one of us. Fuck the humans and the weak Metas who might as well be them, huh?" Slowly, Mai was beginning to regain her equilibrium, and with it came anger strumming gratefully through her veins to steady her hands, her thoughts.

"Despite what you and Denali seem to think, humans are not our concern." Nuala made a gesture as if flicking aside a particularly annoying piece of lint. Her face was granite. "As for your family, we need to make them think they discovered the news of the senator's death on their own. It's useful for us that they think their spies are effective."

Mai nodded, although she was still thinking of how easily Nuala had dismissed the humans. It meant nothing to the enforcer that Absolution had taken dozens of humans and maybe even a few weaker Metas, but now that it was one of them in the morgue, *now* the killer mattered. With her negligible power—at least negligible compared to what her mother and other full-blood Metas could do—Mai was close enough to human that she felt the sting of dismissal like it had been aimed at her own flesh.

She straightened her spine. *Okay.* Despite the body on the ME's table, this wasn't about her. Her family was who she needed to confront, not the enforcers. She thought about the task ahead.

Knowing the skill of the enforcers, the family was likely already aware of Stephen's murder. They were pros at planting information. Her mother liked to think her network of spies was damn near all knowing *and* invisible. Enforcers held the ultimate power of law and justice in the Meta community, but at times, it served their purpose to allow certain Families to think they had some influence within enforcer ranks. Nuala and other enforcers only furthered that notion, making the Families feel self-satisfied and not question how easily they discovered things the enforcers supposedly didn't want them to know.

Only, Mai's life was easy plunder for Mandaia and the family. Other than her shadow life as Mercy, she had no secrets from them, merely illusions of secrecy and of a private life away from her family's all-seeing eye. Knowing that didn't make it any easier to take.

Mai made another move toward the exit, ready to be back in the curated quiet of her own apartment.

Nuala nodded once at her, obviously done with the conversation. "We'll be in touch."

"I look forward to it," Mai said dryly.

She turned to go, but something that had been gnawing at the edge of her consciousness pricked her mouth open.

"I know you want this killer," she began, "but don't you wonder what horrible things my uncle and the other victims did to deserve a death like this?"

"It is not our place to wonder, only to punish."

"Right." Mai pursed her lips. "I'll wait to hear from you then, Enforcer."

Nuala gave another imperious nod, and Mai turned to walk away. With each deliberate step she took from the body rotting in the morgue, the sorrier she felt. Not for herself, but for the murderer who the enforcers would eventually kill. There would be no absolution for him.

CHAPTER 6

ENFORCERS WERE A PAIN IN the ass. Mai almost missed the time when she didn't know much about them beyond what they chose to share, which was little enough. Before that long-ago night when Denali first approached Mai, she had only known the basics: enforcers were recruited at a young age, their members chosen from already-powerful or powerfully intelligent Meta not long after their abilities manifested. The chosen could either accept or refuse the invitation. Their ranks were few but influential, their tactics effective, their decisions final.

After leaving the morgue, Mai made it back home on automatic pilot, taking an Uber instead of the rooftops. Eight o'clock had come and gone, leaving the day bathed in sunlight, so it would've taken too much camouflaging, too much work, to take the roofs back to her condo.

She had the vague idea of getting back into bed and catching some of the sleep Denali's call had stolen from her, but when she let herself into her apartment, the thought of sleep repelled her. After dropping the flash drive with her uncle's autopsy photos and the Absolution case files into a ceramic dish by the door, Mai headed for her sun-filled den.

As she walked, the illusion of clothes peeled back from her body like a receding tide, leaving her bare except for the boy shorts and tank top she'd worn to bed. She settled into the comfortable, overstuffed sofa perfectly placed in the middle of the room for sunlight to fall on her face and throat. But even the sweet burn of sun couldn't stop the thoughts from coming.

Her uncle.

The enforcers.

Her mother.

Mai raked her hands through her hair and loosened the thick coils from their bun, a sigh rippling through her. Sunlight settled into the curves of her face and along her neck, sinking through the thin tank top and into her chest, her breasts, her belly. She turned her face even more into the light.

Five years. Almost two thousand nights and days. Even if she tried, Mai could never forget the night she met Denali and the other enforcers.

It had been an extraordinarily bad night. She'd felt particularly helpless and weak. Her uncle had just won another re-election, and she'd wanted to destroy everything in her path. She wanted to destroy *him*. But instead, she rushed out into the cool November night, her blood boiling.

Mai walked until she nearly couldn't anymore, her legs aching, exhaustion just a breath away. And then she felt it, a thrust of power, and she looked away from the night sky in time to see a dark green SUV fly through the air and then land, roof down, in the cold waters of the Chattahoochee River. Humans screamed, and on the road, a pair of Metas ran on, shoving and playing with each other like children who'd left a broken toy in their wake. They never turned around, and Mai couldn't leave the humans to die.

She pulled the humans from the freezing water to the sound of cell phone cameras going off from onlookers on the riverbank. By the next morning, she'd been christened "Mercy" on YouTube, and videos of her in a hastily created black leather onesie and mask were getting hits all over the world.

Mai had saved those people that night, but she'd also saved herself, diving into the cold and merciless waters of the river to rescue vulnerable humans from careless Meta strength and cruelty, the way she'd wished a thousand times that someone had saved her. As her uncle's re-election proved, the world was intent on elevating men like him, both Meta and human, praising them for being

35

wicked. Mai wanted to *bury* him but brought the human victims up to the water's surface instead. She saved her own humanity, however small it was.

Later that night, as she stood on the roof of her building, Denali, one of three commanders of the North American enforcers, came to her. He'd watched the whole thing unfold in the river, he said. Although it wasn't officially part of his job, he wanted to save humans from Metas too. He asked for Mai's help. In that state of mind, she could only say yes.

Five years later, she was still working with Denali and his enforcers, a secret kept from Mandaia and all the Meta Families worldwide.

Coming back to the present, Mai blinked into the sun, eyes only half-open in order to filter the day's golden light through her lashes. The warmed leather creaked under her shifting body. She drew in a single breath and breathed it out, then fell asleep.

She opened her eyes to darkness, blinking. For a few exquisite moments, her mind swam beneath the shallows of sleep, only concerned with the sensation of soft leather under her nearly naked skin, the lingering warmth from the sun still radiating from the apartment's walls. Then she remembered. Everything.

Mai sat up.

She blinked and saw again her uncle, spread out and opened up beneath the medical examiner's tools. The mingled feelings of relief and then disgust and dread returned in a nauseating flood. Mai pressed a quick hand to her throat.

She had to get out of the apartment.

After a quick shower and change of clothes, she ended up at the café near the university. On a Sunday night, the twenty-four-hour café was still busy. It hummed with conversation and the occasional hiss of the espresso machine, the clink of coffee mugs, and the clicking of laptop keys.

The café was all dark wood and wide windows. It was a comfortable and warm space with the smell of coffee and warm pastries, the familiar sight of students bent over their laptops, and a few couples leaning toward each other at the small tables while their drinks cooled between them.

The café had two bars. One served food and hot drinks, while the other offered only alcohol. Two other people sat at the alcohol bar, where Mai found herself a stool. One was a man with an open letter spread under his limp hand next to a glass of iced white wine that was growing warm while he stared off into space. The other, a woman with her back to Mai, sat sideways as if she were perched on an old-fashioned sidesaddle. She was reading an honest-to-God *paper* copy of a book. Her graceful figure automatically drew Mai's attention, but that wasn't what she'd come to the bar for.

One of the girls who'd been playing with her phone slipped behind the bar and approached Mai.

"Hey, Professor." She greeted Mai with a teasing grin and a pop of her bright-pink chewing gum. It was Beatrice from her Literature in History class. "What can I get for you?"

Today, she was dressed like Harley Quinn from the movie Mai had accidentally seen part of a few months back. Two-toned pigtails, a tight T-shirt with *Monster* scrawled across the chest, sequined panties masquerading as shorts, fishnets, and black Doc Martin boots.

Mai's eyebrows skimmed toward her hairline. "Hello, Beatrice." She didn't look any lower than her student's neck. "I didn't know you worked here."

"There's a lot you don't know about me." The girl leaned on the bar until *Monster* was all but laid out for Mai to pick up.

Mai didn't touch it. "I'm sure," she said. "For now, I'll take a glass of Gewürztraminer, please."

"Sure thing, Prof." Beatrice turned away with a wink to get the wine, aggressively switching her half-covered butt with each step.

When she came back with the wine, glass cold and gleaming with condensation, she leaned over the bar again. "If there's anything I can get for you just…" and the cheeky girl actually laughed at herself. "…put your lips together and blow." She giggled and popped her gum.

"I'll keep that in mind," Mai said, absolutely confident she wouldn't blow anything within ten miles of that child.

After Beatrice sashayed away to serve another customer, Mai turned her attentions to her drink.

The crisp, sweet wine had barely touched her tongue when a nearby voice said, "Are you another one of those?"

The tone of the words, and the sense of scorn they carried, surprised Mai into looking up. She bumped into the hard gaze of Xóchitl Bentley.

"Excuse me?" Mai narrowed her eyes at the woman who sat, sleek and untouchable, one stool over. In her attempts to stay away from Xóchitl, she'd never spoken to her before, to her occasional regret. She'd looked her fill plenty, but aside from a few brief words at the odd departmental meeting, she hadn't had much opportunity to hear her speak.

"Are you gonna take that kid home and *fuck* her in exchange for giving her an A?" The curse was jarring, tossed at her from a near stranger. "That's the question I'm asking."

Xóchitl Bentley's antagonism shocked Mai like a slap. She looked at the woman from the top of her perfectly styled hair to the pointed toes of her designer shoes. She felt her face go hard, the bones sharpening under the layers of muscle, tissue, and skin. Her eyes felt like flint.

Her first instinct was to dismiss the other professor and her insulting question by ignoring her and going back to her wine. It was, after all, a question that showed Xóchitl Bentley really didn't know who she was talking to. But after dealing with her uncle on the slab, and the feelings the sight of him brought up, she felt emptied of her normal responses.

Her back stiffened, and she looked the woman over again, this time with a slow and insulting once-over that missed nothing, certainly not the slender body artfully displayed in an oversized, boatneck dress that paradoxically emphasized the beguiling shape of her. The graceful head and short haircut accentuated the regal tilt of her chin, her long neck, and the exclamation points of her collarbones.

Xóchitl Bentley adjusted herself on the stool under Mai's gaze, and the collection of thin bracelets on each arm chimed dimly. She looked like a queen, and despite Mai's now-aggressive stance, Xóchitl's question made her feel like a dung-covered peasant.

"If I had planned on doing exactly that, do you want to intervene and offer yourself in her place?" The venom of the question spilled easily off Mai's tongue.

Xóchitl was absolutely poised, just as Mai expected her to be. If it hadn't been for the slight twitch of the hand on her book, Mai would've thought she hadn't even heard her. Xóchitl shifted again on the stool, and her scent, vanilla and oranges, reached Mai.

"If that girl is what you like, I doubt you'd know what to do with a *real* woman."

"Is that what you are? I couldn't tell with you sitting there like an ice queen judging someone you don't know from high up on your throne."

"I've heard enough about you to form my own judgments."

Mai raised an eyebrow, an unspoken gesture for the woman to go ahead and regale her with everything she'd heard that had helped form her judgments. But Xóchitl Bentley only shrugged and went back to her book, leaving Mai to seethe in her own anger. She was vaguely aware of the man near them stirring out of his stupor to look in their direction.

Her fury wouldn't let her stay quiet. "It's interesting that someone who is a professor of feminism and theory would allow petty campus gossip to inform her judgments about another woman, a stranger."

"So you *do* know who I am."

"Just as you apparently know who I am," Mai said with a sarcastic bite. She settled more comfortably on her stool and sipped the crisp sweetness of her wine, but it immediately turned sour in her mouth.

"Did I hear you whistle, Professor?"

She almost didn't hear when Beatrice slipped back behind the bar, fragile and human with her persistent flirtation that Xóchitl

Bentley had apparently interpreted as signs of an ongoing affair between them. Strangely, the woman's assumptions made her want to prove something. What, precisely? She didn't quite know.

"Not unless you interpret my intense desire for a real drink as a whistle, love." *What the fuck are you doing?*

Even as she spoke to her student, altering her body language to suit seduction instead of professorial distance, Beatrice stiffened, eyelashes fluttering in confusion as if she didn't know what to do with this different version of her professor. Mai didn't blame her. She needed to leave this place before she did something truly stupid.

The girl's confusion—and backpedaling—were hilariously obvious, but Mai didn't have it in her to laugh. Was that all she'd needed to do for Beatrice to back off? Just pretend to take her up on one of her endless offers? Good to know for the future.

"You know what? Forget about that drink. How much do I owe you?"

Beatrice stammered out an amount, and Mai dropped enough money on the bar to cover that plus a fifty-percent tip. "Thanks. I'll see you next week."

Christ! It sounded like she was talking about meeting her in their private fuck palace on a prearranged date. Mai stuck the rest of her folded bills inside her jacket pocket and stood up to leave.

"Professor Redstone…" Xóchitl Bentley called her name, her voice not quite as cool before, but Mai was done listening to her. She tipped her head Beatrice's way, then left the café, her boot heels ringing against the hardwood floors. Outside, she ducked into a quiet side street.

Mai was furious. The anger settled cold and hot at the same time in her chest, wreaking havoc with her self-control. Other feelings writhed inside her too, but the anger was the easiest one to focus on. As she walked from the café on the lamp-lit streets, her skin prickled with that rage, muscles twitching and shifting under her face, showing different features to the few people she passed in the small downtown side streets before shifting back to a neutral mask. The anger made her literally shake in her boots.

She desperately needed to settle. She desperately needed calm. Mai drew in a deep and trembling breath and reached out with her senses.

A wild and sudden siren snared her hearing. Sharp and long, the sound sawed along her nerves like sharp teeth, high and strident enough that it could have come from a truck or an ambulance. But as soon as she heard it, Mai knew it was a person made the sound. A person in pain.

And it was far enough away that she would have to *hurry, hurry, hurry* to get there, but it was the perfect excuse she needed to get away from the café and Xóchitl and the feelings she'd brought up in Mai. The pain had felt too familiar. Like it came from Family. So she ran.

Her steps rapped against the concrete, and the wind slapped her face, tearing at her eyes before she made a slight adjustment to her lids. Then she was silently scaling the side of the big marble building near the university, and there, *there,* she could run her full speed and let the thrill of the impending confrontation heat her blood.

Mercy is coming.

When she got there, she saw sadness. A woman sprawled on the side of the dark road, legs at odd angles and her skirt halfway up her thighs. She sobbed into a cell to 911 while the phone's dying battery ticked away like a time bomb.

"My car!" The woman screamed into the beeping phone like her world was ending. "They took my car!"

She wasn't telling them the rest, too caught up in the pain and panic. But Mai had already seen the child car seat in the back of the white Honda as it swerved around the corner, much too far away for the woman to follow. But it wasn't too far for Mai. After a quick squeeze of the woman's shoulder, she chased after them.

Music blared from the car over the lashing tide of triumphant and boyish laughter as a heavy foot gave even more gas to the car. In the back seat, the child was still, incredibly, sleeping.

She ran faster.

The boys—because they were just boys—found a station they liked and cranked it up even higher until the music, loud death metal, drowned out everything but the sound of their laughter and the clatter of them tossing things out the window: CDs, a hairbrush, a pink glass water bottle that shattered in the street, leaving a wet stain that Mai jumped over. The baby woke and started to cry.

As the boys raced the car down the street, there were trees and quiet houses tucked away behind hedges and TV lights flickering behind pulled curtains. A few curtains twitched to the side when the noise of their passing came, but those curtains quickly fell back into place as if nothing had disturbed them.

Mai ran and ran.

Up ahead, the car roared along the small two-lane road. Behind her, the woman continued to scream into the phone, but her phone was already dead.

The boys didn't know what to do. Mai could see it all as she chased them. And the moment they discovered the baby in the back seat, the car swerved across the lanes in shock. Then they saw her, the whites of their eyes flashing upward in the rearview mirror. They pushed the car even faster, trying to outrun Mai's shadowy form.

But Mercy was coming for them.

"We need to get rid of it!" The boys shouted at each other in the car.

"That chick is out there. She'll turn us in to the cops!"

The car sped farther away, and music banged through its metal cage, vicious and loud. The baby wailed along under the chorus, panicked and angry. Or maybe just hungry. But the boys' luck, such as it was, wouldn't hold for long. Up ahead was construction. A small bridge. They wouldn't survive the fall if they kept swerving and arguing and not paying attention to what was in front of them.

"There's a fuckin' baby in here, man!" The boys kept at it. "That's kidnapping or some shit!"

"You shoulda thought of that when you had this fucking bright idea to jack the car."

"Me?" And it went on.

Over a mile away behind them now, the woman on the ground was hysterical. The child screamed nearly as loudly as its mother. The two boys argued. The bridge came closer.

Mai ran even faster. Faster. Then jumped.

She landed on top of the car with a thud. The impact knocked the air from her lungs. The residual heat of the day that had absorbed into the roof immediately sank through her clothes and into her bare chest. She smashed her fist through the windshield. The glass shattered, and Mai grabbed the edge of the open driver's side window to catch herself from immediately sliding off.

"Stop the car," she growled, pitching her voice for the boys to hear her above the music and the screaming baby.

The driver only sped up.

"Try to throw her off!" the brilliant sidekick suggested, eyes dilated with fear and some sort of drug Mai didn't bother to smell for.

"This isn't the movies, dude!"

But his friend made a frantic grab for the wheel and jerked the car from one side of the street to the other, flicking his eyes between Mai and the road in front of him. The driver elbowed his friend in the face and wrestled the wheel from his hands, and the car swerved again, slinging Mai to the other side of the roof. She slid along the roof and gritted her teeth from the pain that shot through her arms as she held on. She hissed at the abrupt pull and burn in her muscles but couldn't afford to let go. The child would pay too high of a price. The mother would be destroyed. Mai would never forgive herself.

She grunted with the effort of holding on as the car barreled down the street, clipping bushes and shrubs when it veered too close to the edge of the road. A twig dug into her cheek as it flew past, and she hissed from this new pain.

Car tires screeched against the pavement, and the bridge was barreling closer, too narrow to withstand the extreme jerking of the car. The boys seemed too focused on getting Mai off the roof to pay proper attention to just how dangerous the bridge was. She had to get them to stop the car before the bridge.

Mai dove to the side and reached into the car to yank the steering wheel at the same time as the explosive sound of a bullet rocked the inside the car.

"What the fuck?" one of the boys shouted in shock.

The baby screamed even louder. Mai's hand grabbed hold of the wheel the moment she realized a bullet hole had torn through the car roof, splitting through the space where her body had been seconds before. The car screeched to a stop, nearly throwing Mai forward and into the street. The momentum grabbed at her arms again, and she used it to catapult herself up and over, landing on her feet in front of the stopped car.

"Are you out of your fuckin' mind?" The rest of what the driver screamed was incoherent and panicked, his cries nearly as high as the child's. He sounded like he was hyperventilating, his quick breaths making the car nearly as hot as the gun smoking from the hand of his accomplice, who looked wild-eyed, as if he hadn't truly known what it meant to truly fire a weapon.

Before they could get their scattered shit together, Mai jumped onto the hood of the car, taking them both by surprise and smashing the windshield with the sharp drive of her fist. Glass showered down onto the hood, onto the street, and was still showering down around her when Mai shoved herself into the car and grabbed the boy's gun hand. She twisted and squeezed, breaking the small bones in his wrist and hand.

He screamed. Mai caught the other boy with a slashing elbow across the face, breaking his nose. Another slam of her fist slumped him back into the seat, unconscious. The car smelled like sweat and baby vomit, fear and old marijuana.

Screams still rattled the car. The baby. The boy with the gun. Or who once had the gun. The semiautomatic was heavy, warm, and ugly in Mai's gloved hand. She ejected the clip and emptied the chamber while the screaming boy watched her with terrified eyes and shrunk back into the seat. The rage built in Mai. It swept through her in waves and was hot enough to kill.

"Leave me alone!" he roared at her, cradling his broken hand. "I'm gonna tell the cops what you did. You can't treat me like this. I have rights!"

The baby screamed louder at the boy's shouts. Mai didn't want to hear either of them anymore. The shooter's mouth opened wide enough for her to see the unfilled cavities at the back of his mouth.

"Shut up." Mai slammed her head into his, and he fell abruptly silent, fell back into the seat like an abandoned marionette, a twin to his friend in the driver's seat.

One screamer down, one to go.

She yanked the key from the ignition and shoved it into her pocket, then twisted herself into the back seat, where the baby wailed from beneath the swaddle of pink blankets. The child's face was hot under the tender brush of Mai's hand, her cheeks wet with tears, nose dripping. With uncertain fingers, Mai unlatched the child from the car seat and, making the shushing noises she'd seen other people do with children in distress, climbed from the car with the gradually quieting bundle in her arms.

She could still hear the crying mother and, distantly, the sound of sirens. Shaking in the aftermath of the adrenaline rush, Mai held the child against her chest and began the long walk to where a mother was waiting to see her child safe.

CHAPTER 7

SHE WAS STILL SHAKING WHEN she climbed through the window of her condo. It was a good kind of tremor, though, her muscles sore from having done something good with the small amount of power she had. Someone had been glad to see her. Had welcomed her presence.

With a grunt, Mai tugged off her boots and put them away. Her feet tapped, quiet and bare, against the glossy wooden floors of her bedroom, and she felt the suppleness of her body, the strength in it. Its utility. She stripped and dropped her clothes into the laundry hamper just outside the bathroom door.

Naked, she closed the clear door of the shower behind her and nearly sagged with pleasure under the hot spray. The long afternoon with the family, the shock of her uncle's lifeless body in the morgue, Xóchitl Bentley's unexpected venom: all those things had disappeared while she'd worn Mercy's mask. Her sigh was mingled relief and exhaustion as she braced her arms against the tiled shower walls and let the scalding water rush over her head and back.

Nearly an hour later, she opened the bathroom door, and steam billowed out ahead of her. As she dried her hair, she stepped into her bedroom.

"If I were that kind, I could have killed you a thousand times over tonight."

Mai felt like she'd been doused in a bucket of cold water. Her mother, who'd never visited her place before, stood in her bedroom, the leather jacket and gloves she'd worn as Mercy held in one hand.

"How can you presume to protect these humans when you can't even protect yourself?" Her mother looked like shattered glass in Mai's private space, glittering and dangerous. The smiling TV personality and philanthropist she presented to the rest of the world was gone, the mask discarded in favor of her real self. After a scornful look at the clothes in her hand, she dropped them back into the laundry basket.

Mai's heart beat wildly in her chest like a rabbit caught in a trap. To keep some of her terror at bay, Mai scrubbed the towel through her hair one last time, then headed for her walk-in closet, all the while keeping her shoulders back and spine straight, wearing her nudity like armor. "To what do I owe this absolute pleasure, Mother?"

Dammit. But her mother being there could only mean one thing. Mai pulled sweatpants and a tank top from her dresser, then sat down on the bed, still nude, to massage lotion into her skin. From the corner of her eye, she watched Mandaia, still wary, although she pretended not to be.

"Your Uncle Stephen is dead," she said. "But I'm sure you know that already."

Mai flinched, her fingers digging for a moment into her calves with the spread of the sweet-smelling rose-and-eucalyptus lotion that always signaled bedtime for her. The lotion was one she'd used since she was in high school, but suddenly the scent was too much in the same room with her mother. It rose up, too sweet, threatening to choke her. She swallowed quickly to stop herself from gagging.

"Find out who did this to Stephen. Bring the murderer to us." Her mother's eyes flashed a dangerous gold, her version of grief.

"Why should I turn them in to you and not an enforcer?" Mai asked the question although she already knew the answer. "They're better equipped to deal with something like this."

"An enforcer wouldn't allow for the kind of justice the family demands," her mother said.

Mai clenched her teeth until her jaw hurt. Mandaia and her lackeys planned on torturing the killer the same way the killer had tortured Stephen. *If* they ever got their hands on Absolution. Denali and the others would never allow it.

"Make this happen," Mandaia continued, her voice cold and resolute. "This means catching the killer and bringing them to us takes priority over your little hobby with the enforcers. Am I clear?"

Of *course* she knew about Mercy and Mai's work with the enforcers. Any illusions Mai had about possessing even one of her own secrets were just that. "Crystal clear."

The last time Mai had disobeyed an order from her mother, she'd lost a job she loved, along with most of her friends. Disobedience in something like this wasn't an option. She thought of her students at the university, her recent tenure, the glimmerings of a life she'd built away from the Family.

Unable to stand the smell of the lotion anymore, Mai capped the bottle and put it carefully on the bedside table. Her skin shuddered under the scum of the lotion. She jerked to her feet. "I'd like to get dressed now, if you please. We don't know each other well enough for me to get dressed in your company."

At first, she thought her mother would protest and insist on staying out of spite. But she turned another significant look onto Mai, then walked out of the bedroom. Mai waited until she heard the click of the front door, counted to ten past that, then rushed to the bathroom.

The metal trash can rang dully from the slam of the nearly full bottle of lotion. In the shower again, she scrubbed her skin until it burned and all traces of the lotion were gone. Another thing her mother had ruined for her.

Mai put her mother's trespass out of her mind because she had to. She'd had years of practice tucking away the hurts her family slung her way in order to focus on less painful things. No matter who she ultimately gave the information to, she had to find out who killed her uncle.

In her home office, she lay the files and photographs across her desk and studied them until her eyes burned. The victims were varied. A priest, a psychiatrist, a couple of teachers, a few midlevel office workers. All ordinary-seeming people except for her uncle.

Nine women. Thirty-seven murders total, over six years. Three of them in Atlanta. The numbers spun in her head. On the surface of it, nothing linked all the victims. Not region. Not habits. Not gender. Criminal records for nearly all of them were nonexistent. They lived all over the country, and six of them lived abroad most of the year. But going by her own experience with her uncle, Mai knew what to look for:

Frequent hospital visits from younger or weaker people in their lives. Large sums of money disappearing from their bank accounts—possible abuse victim payoffs. Past suspicion of abuse or violence. Restraining orders. For every murder victim, she was able to check off two of the signs, sometimes all four, until the evidence of what they all had in common was unavoidable and all the information clicked neatly into place to form a pattern.

But she had to be sure.

The following week, back at work, the abuse victims' faces and those of their murdered abusers still swirled through her mind as she made her way down the hallway toward her office at the university. She was distracted. That was the reason she didn't hear it the first time someone called her name. Or the second. It was the hand on her arm, a touch that came from behind, that pulled her thoughts and attentions back to the here and now.

"Professor Redstone."

Mai turned, masking her annoyance with a generic smile. Which faded as soon as she saw who it was. The hand fell away.

"Professor Bentley." A muscle ticked in Mai's jaw, and she consciously loosened the tight clench of her teeth. But her smile stayed gone.

Despite her annoyance and aroused anger, Mai wasn't blind. Xóchitl Bentley was stunning in beige slacks, loose and flowing like water over her hips, and a thin, white blouse buttoned all the way to her throat. She looked like a present waiting to be unwrapped. The thought made Mai curl her lip at herself in disgust.

Xóchitl took a small step back, and it seemed a steadying movement rather than a retreat.

"What can I do for you?" Mai asked when the woman didn't seem inclined to get to the point.

"I…" Long hands slid into the pockets of her slacks, and the gaze Xóchitl turned on Mai became blatantly confrontational. "I want to apologize."

"For what?" She refused to believe the woman thought any differently of her than she had a few days before.

"I jumped to conclusions about you and that student…Beatrice. And about a few other things too. I was wrong."

Mai frowned. "And how did you reach this great clarity?"

"You can't take an apology, can you?"

"I can take an apology just fine. It's tricks and bullshit that I don't accept so easily."

"No tricks. No bullshit." Xóchitl Bentley held up her hands in a pose of surrender. "Beatrice wasn't very sweet to me after you left the other night. She defended you like you were her child…or her mother."

Mai raised an eyebrow. "And that didn't make you believe your assumptions even more?"

"Strangely enough, no." She dipped her head then, looking a bit embarrassed. "That might have something to do with the gentleman sitting next to me who just about asked me if I was insane for saying those things to you. In his mind, you're apparently one of the few teachers on campus who *doesn't* prey on students."

"Okay." Because what else could Mai say in response to that? She knew how she conducted herself at the university. She damn sure didn't need anyone who wasn't her boss to validate her behavior.

"Okay, then."

Then that seemed to be it, because Xóchitl Bentley said nothing else. For long seconds, she looked content to simply gaze in Mai's face, a slight smile on her lips.

Mai stared back in bemusement, reluctantly appreciating all over again the symmetry of the woman's face, the curve of her mouth, the slow and measured breathing that barely disturbed the white silk over her breasts. Mai tucked the tip of her tongue into the corner of her mouth as she dropped her gaze to, then away from, the insides of Xóchitl's elbows, beguiling indents of flesh just under the thin fabric of her blouse. They were places that seemed made for Mai's fingers, for the curious brush of her mouth.

Mai cleared her throat and took a step back. "Well, that was nice." She gripped the handle of her briefcase. "Thanks for that… whatever it was. I'll see you around." She turned to go, but Xóchitl grabbed her arm again. Mai froze.

The fingers on her arm tightened briefly before letting go. "Can I see you this evening after class?" Xóchitl asked.

"Why?"

"To buy you a drink. I don't think my verbal apology convinced you enough."

"I don't need convincing."

"But maybe *I* do."

Mai dropped her eyes down the woman's body again, trying to sense more than see what she was about. The odd cloth bag she'd carried with her every time Mai had seen her was held loosely in front of her in both hands. She looked like a fashion model stuck holding her hippie sister's book bag.

The attraction she felt for the woman, along with the anger from their last—and only—conversation, stirred an unfamiliar and unwelcome bittersweet at the back of Mai's throat. She wasn't used to feeling this way. And certainly not about a human. The unpleasant cocktail raised her hackles and made her want to lash out. But this wasn't the place. Her job was sacred to her in a way that few understood; sometimes even she didn't understand it but only knew that it took the place of family in her life, was comforting in a way that nothing else was—not even the restful glass box in the sky she called her apartment.

"Okay," Mai finally responded, surprising herself. "One drink."

After Xóchitl finally allowed her to leave, she went on to her office, then to classes, now doubly distracted.

In the name of starting fresh, they'd agreed to meet at a bar far enough from campus and closer to Mai's condo. She had time to drop off her briefcase and nearly chicken out of the meeting (not date) while standing in her living room with a hand on the doorknob. But in the end, she went.

The sound of Rihanna's "Desperado" greeted her as she walked into the crowded restaurant and bar, warm with its human smells, competing perfumes, and artisanal alcohol extracted from random roots and berries. This was more the type of place her brother would like, written up in the local papers and boasting a dozen types of mayonnaise.

To distance herself from the strange idea that it might be a date, Mai kept on her "professor clothes," minus the blazer she usually wore to protect herself against the school's arctic air-conditioning. She'd barely made it inside the door, smelling the air and wondering what the hell she was doing so far outside her comfort zone, when Xóchitl emerged from the bar. And *emerged* was the only way to put it when she seemed to part the crowd of standing patrons with her slender frame, a hand lifted to wave Mai her way. It was 9:30 p.m. on the dot.

"Thank you for coming. I was worried you wouldn't make it."

Mai shrugged. She wasn't responsible for the woman's worries. "Are we sitting inside or out?"

"Outside, if you don't mind. I love the weather this time of year." She shocked Mai by taking her hand, warm and strong, and pulling her through the crowd.

Outside, their table was set for two and settled on a terrace overlooking a Japanese-style garden, complete with a minimalist water fountain trickling tranquility into the night air. The terrace was only big enough for three tables with two chairs each, so with the doors closed, it was quieter out there. Intimate.

The other tables were occupied, but the couples were deeply involved in their own quiet conversations. Their voices barely raised above a whisper.

They sat down.

"I took the liberty of ordering for you," Xóchitl said. "I remembered you were drinking a white wine the other day."

As she finished speaking, a waitress arrived with a tray bearing a bowl of sliced strawberries, a bottle of wine, and two glasses. She greeted Mai with a smile and her soft voice, settling the wine on the table and pouring a small measure of it for Xóchitl to taste and approve. Mai watched the performance with a jaundiced look. It was something she'd seen her mother do a hundred times at most meals—whether business or personal—her presence so powerful that servers invariably gave her the wine to taste and approve without considering anyone else at the table. Mai didn't mind. Power wasn't something she was invested in.

After the wine performance was over, she sat back with her poured but untouched glass of white wine to watch Xóchitl.

"Thank you for coming."

"You said that already," Mai said.

"It bears mentioning again, doesn't it?"

Mai shrugged. And was a little surprised when Xóchitl's eyes blatantly followed the movement of her breasts beneath the starched buttoned-up shirt.

As if reading her mind—or likely her uncharacteristically open expression—Xóchitl said, "You're very beautiful. No wonder more than half your students are in love with you."

"And that made you assume I'm sleeping with them?" To stop herself from fidgeting, Mai settled her fingers around the stem of her wineglass.

"They're so very tempting, aren't they?" Xóchitl bit into a strawberry and slowly chewed.

"They're children. Like you said, if I wanted someone to fuck, I'd choose a woman who could properly say no to me without worrying I'd tank her grade."

Xóchitl winced. "I'm really sorry about that."

"Why?"

"Because it's the right thing to be in a situation like this. And because I was wrong."

But it didn't feel that simple. There was something else at play here. Whatever it was, Xóchitl didn't seem in a hurry to let her know. Mai could play along, though. She'd had enough experience doing that with her family. Playing possum.

"Okay." She picked up her glass and waved the faintly fruity wine under her nose. "Tell me, what are we drinking?"

Xóchitl's face brightened with a sudden smile, an alarming thing to see on someone usually so cold, at least in Mai's limited experience. She hid her unease by sipping her wine and nodding to feign interest when Xóchitl rattled off the wine's country of birth and reasons to pay more than ten dollars for it.

"Sounds nice enough." She looked around the terrace and through the glass doors into the rest of the restaurant. The hipster crowd was mostly in its twenties and thirties. No one she recognized. If Xóchitl had invited her to this place to keep her off-balance, it wasn't quite working. One set of humans at a drinking hole was very much like another, whether they were in her neighborhood, by the university, or in a BDSM club.

Xóchitl's hand reached across the table to grip hers, and she flinched from its warmth, so much like her own. The touch felt too comfortable. "Don't drift away," she said to Mai, her eyes cool and hot at once.

Mai shook her head and tried not to squirm from Xóchitl's touch. "You're here to apologize to me, not make demands, remember?" She *had* been mentally drifting away from this woman she had the most unfortunate attraction to. It was self-preservation more than anything else. Although if she'd truly wanted to save herself, she wouldn't have agreed to this ridiculous so-called apology in the first place.

Unable to take it anymore, Mai pulled her hand back. "This wasn't a good idea." She pushed back from the table. "Consider yourself forgiven. I'll see you at school."

Xóchitl leapt to her feet and blocked Mai's way out. "Please. Stay."

"Why?"

She didn't see the kiss coming. And if she had seen it, Mai wasn't sure she would've done anything to avoid it. The press of Xóchitl's mouth against hers was a quick, warm suction that stole all the breath from Mai's lungs. She backed away, but Xóchitl followed with the soft temptation of her mouth. Where the restaurant had been a vague hum around her before, it suddenly became a roar of voices, a wave of sound rising over her, overwhelming.

Then everything was silent, all sound gone. And she simply *felt.*

The hammering of her heart. Xóchitl's hot mouth. The rush of superheated blood under her cheeks. Her hands tingled with the desire to touch. Then it was more than a desire, and she *was* touching Xóchitl, gripping her waist and parting her lips to accept and double the kiss, greedily licking the taste of crisp wine and strawberries from Xóchitl's mouth.

Then Xóchitl pulled away, and it was Mai's turn to follow and keep the connection between their bodies.

"We should..." Xóchitl's voice was low and rough, her breath hot against Mai's cheek. "We should probably take this someplace more private."

With the sound of her voice came other sounds: tittering laughter from one of the tables nearby, voices, people whispering about them. Then came the awareness that she'd been practically feeling up Xóchitl on the terrace. Mai liked sex as much as anyone else, but she didn't like it in public, and she definitely didn't like when the feelings associated with it—overheated desperation, panties damp with lust, her breath shallowing like she was fighting for air—snuck up on her and left her just shy of a panic attack.

Shit.

"I should go," she said. "Alone."

If she stayed any longer in Xóchitl's presence, her slight loss of control would become total, her humiliation complete. She walked as quickly out of the restaurant as she could without actually running. Her hand was in her pocket and on her keys when she heard Xóchitl behind her, felt the urgency of her pursuit. Mai unlocked the car door, but before she could slide inside, warm hands grasped her waist and spun her around as if there was no resistance in her at all. She had been resisting, right?

"Don't go."

Xóchitl was telling her something else. Her body sensed it in the delicate tremors flooding through her at the woman's very presence. This entire encounter felt *off* somehow. Had she done something? Changed herself in some way she hadn't realized? She tried desperately to remember. But she couldn't.

"I don't do this," Mai said. She was pathetically grateful for the steadiness of her voice.

"Do what?"

That was a good question. She slept with women whom she barely knew all the time. That was how she preferred it, as close to anonymous as she could get—only bodies shared for a moment— nothing else that could be taken for real intimacy.

Xóchitl was too close. Her breath. Her smell. Mai tried to summon enough anger to push her away, but all she felt was magnetized, pulled inexorably forward. Her stomach dipped, and the want roared through her like an actual fire, scorching any of her remaining senses.

Then they were kissing again, Mai pressed between Xóchitl's body and the open driver's side of the car. It felt good. So damn good. The bleeding away of her mind's endless calculations and concerns left in their place the wants of her body, its drive to devour and burn and taste and grab every bit of pleasure from the moment.

Xóchitl made a sound like pain, like she'd been struck in the stomach—a puff of breath, her gasp into Mai's mouth a moment before she gripped the back of Mai's neck, her fingers sinking into skin. She deepened the kiss, sucking on Mai's tongue, licking and biting like there was something in Mai's mouth that she absolutely needed in order to survive.

She gripped Mai's ass and lifted with an effortless strength that made Mai gasp and grab the edge of the car door. But there was no need for her to worry about falling, at least not in that way, because Xóchitl had her. She pushed Mai's back against the solid edge of the car, one hand firmly on her ass, the other blindly pushing up her skirt. Her fingers rubbed the already-damp crotch of Mai's panties, and Mai groaned into the hot mouth on hers, already abandoning the grip on the car to grab onto Xóchitl and spread her own thighs wider for the firmer stroke of the woman's fingers.

Those fingers slipped past the damp cloth of her panties and into wetness—over Mai's clit. She bucked in Xóchitl's hold. Pleasure lanced through her like danger, activating her fight-or-flight response, but there was nowhere to go. The pleasure surrounded her, crowded her in the form of Xóchitl's too-warm body, the waves of sensation coursing through her from the contact points between them.

"Oh God…"

She was dripping and falling back against the roof of the car, her hips moving with the confident stroke of Xóchitl's fingers. She felt them over her slick wetness, heard the moist kiss of them moving on her, then *inside* her. The breath shuddered in her throat. Heat and pleasure burst from the movement of Xóchitl's fingers, from that place of incendiary contact, and then Mai was crying out her bliss into the warm evening. Her body clutched and shuddered in Xóchitl's embrace, her panties soaked and her thighs trembling. Slowly, Xóchitl lowered her to her feet.

Her face looked as shocked as Mai felt.

"Take me home with you," Xóchitl whispered. Her kisses landed on Mai's parted and panting lips, on her cheek, her jaw, the side of her neck. "I'll be so good to you in a bed."

Although Mai couldn't speak, not with the breath running away from her like this, her body was already giving its permission, swaying toward Xóchitl and weeping a yes from between her legs.

But a flash of a camera phone trained on them brought her mind abruptly back to reality. She cleared her throat, smoothed her skirt back down her thighs, and turned abruptly away from the camera and the two men chuckling a few feet away.

Xóchitl growled when she looked over her shoulder and noticed the men. Mai thought for a moment that her eyes flashed a dangerous silver. But it must have been another blast of light from the camera phone's flash.

"I can't." She licked her swollen lips and tasted the already-fading flavor of Xóchitl. "I need to go."

Then, before her body could betray her again, she slipped into the small gap between the open door and Xóchitl's body and dropped down into the car. She started the engine, forcing the woman to step back before she slammed the door shut, and drove out of the parking lot. Her fingers stayed tightly locked around the steering wheel during the entire drive home.

When she got back to her apartment, she was no clearer on what had just happened. Her mind felt scattered to the four winds, and even the cold shower couldn't purge the memory of Xóchitl's hands between her legs, the soft breath on her skin, her sharp teeth grazing the side of Mai's neck as Xóchitl panted, "Come for me," just before Mai gratefully did what she commanded.

It took her hours to finally fall asleep.

The next day, Mai was a wreck. With every bite of food she took, she swore she tasted Xóchitl on her tongue. Every time she took deep a breath, the familiar scent of vanilla and oranges ghosted through her senses. At one point, she even thought she saw Xóchitl near her condo. But she knew those were all illusions, just as she knew nothing would come of whatever it was they were playing at.

She was still angry at the woman for the way she had treated her in the bar a few nights before. But the need to reject her wasn't there anymore. Instead, she wanted to taste her again, to feel what it would be like to make love to her in a bed. But that wasn't an option for them. Despite their mutual attraction, she didn't shit where she ate.

A workplace romance would be a disaster.

So Mai talked herself out of having anything to do with Xóchitl, other than the occasional hello in the hallway.

Less than a week after the parking lot mistake, Mai approached the end of her last class of the day with a bone-deep sigh of relief. She had a lead to follow on the Absolution case and already felt a thrum of excitement at the pursuit, even though she wouldn't be able to start until the next afternoon.

She was getting closer to Absolution; she could feel it. Even though with that growing proximity, she wasn't sure if she wanted to capture or congratulate them.

"I don't think it's instructive to lump the slavery practiced on the African continent with the forms it took in the United States, the Caribbean, and South America," one of her students was saying.

"Why not? It's all slavery! You can't pick and choose which one you support and which one you condemn."

The rush of antagonism in the class brought Mai back to the discussion that was rapidly in danger of becoming a fistfight rather than an intellectual debate.

Mai flicked her gaze to the clock at the back of the room. Fifteen minutes until the end of class. "I think that's enough lively conversation," she said, tapping a pen against her knee and giving a firm look to the two students leaning toward each other in blatant hostility. "This is not a history class, everyone. But feel free to put your paper on the novel into a historical context, remembering that we are discussing the literature and not indulging in our not-so-latent racist or xenophobic tendencies. Okay?" She raised a pointed eyebrow, and the some of the students had the good sense to look embarrassed.

The classroom door creaked open, but Mai didn't bother to look who it was. Probably a student from the next class who didn't realize how early they were. She looked at the clock again. "We have another ten minutes, so if someone else wants to present the topic of their paper to us, let's have it."

But most of the students were looking over Mai's shoulder. Beatrice, in particular, looked like she wanted to strangle whoever it was she was looking at. Mai sighed, turning around. "We're not done…" Her words fell away when she saw who it was.

Xóchitl sat in a chair close to the door as if she intended to stay a while. Mai flushed, then immediately tried to look like she hadn't.

She turned back to face her students, but no one volunteered to talk about their paper. They were suddenly playing shy. Mai cleared her throat. "Why don't we call it a night? Send your proposals to me by midnight tomorrow, and we'll go from there."

While she talked, most of the students stared at Xóchitl with naked curiosity, obviously wondering who she was and why she felt so free to interrupt Mai's class. Or more importantly, why Mai allowed the interruption. All she knew was that she couldn't focus while Xóchitl watched her. The back of her neck tingled with awareness and with a familiar warmth that flowed down her spine and settled into her hips.

Mai pursed her lips, annoyed at her own reaction. "Good night, good night," she said, waving her students toward the door with her glasses. "E-mail me or Carol with any questions you have."

For a wild moment, none of them moved. Then Mai stood up. "That was your not-so-subtle cue to scram. You don't have to go home, but you can't stay here." She smiled crookedly at their nosiness, absolutely *not* looking behind her.

The stampede of students quickly started, but it seemed to take them forever to actually leave. Beatrice stood in a circle with three of her friends, a small stack of books pressed against her chest and her eyes shooting daggers at Xóchitl. Mai internally sighed and dropped her glasses into her briefcase. She slung the slim leather case over her shoulder and walked toward Xóchitl.

"What can I do for you, Dr. Bentley?"

Xóchitl was composure itself, immaculate in a white, 1950s-style dress with a wide, black belt and high-heeled black shoes. Her lipstick was very red. She flicked a gaze behind Mai, the corner of her mouth ticking up at the sight of Beatrice, who wasn't being subtle at all about her annoyance. Or jealousy.

"Walk with me?"

Mai pressed her lips briefly together and had a flash of sense memory, the taste of Xóchitl on her tongue. "Sure."

They walked down the hallway, the heels of their shoes tapping against the tile floors, hollow and loud. Mai didn't know what there was to say after the last time they saw each other. Those moments were seared into her mind and into her skin, possibly for a very, very long time. But that didn't mean anything, did it?

Their footsteps took them toward the courtyard just outside the building that housed their offices. Swaying trees whispered in the delicate night breeze, offering shelter and shadow and only a faint respite from the heat. The weather was perfect.

"You're not what I expected," Xóchitl said as they rounded a curve on the path.

Starlight and lamplight glowed above them and settled on the cool curves of her face. The tilt of her mouth was like a question.

"You mean because I don't sleep with my students?"

"No, that was—" Xóchitl cut herself off, slid her hands into the pockets of her dress, and seemed to really think about what she meant. "You're not like the others, and…you're actually kind of nice."

"Nice?" Mai almost laughed. No one ever said that about her.

Some of her laughter must have leaked through her voice, because Xóchitl huffed softly. "I said *kind of* nice."

This time, Mai did laugh. "Wait until you really get to know me."

"I'd actually like that." Xóchitl's voice went low. "To really get to know you."

Mai's laughter died. She bit the inside of her lip, strangely reluctant to say what she already knew. If—when—their fascination with each other ended, being around each other would become damn near unbearable. Her job, her refuge, would become tainted. Shitting and eating. No.

"I don't think that's a good idea," she said.

Xóchitl stopped on the path and turned. "Give me one good reason why not." Her brown eyes, warming under the burn of the moon and stars, drew Mai in until it felt like she was leaning in, waiting to be kissed and devoured as she had that night in the restaurant parking lot.

But Mai held herself back. Barely. She had so many reasons for them not to see each other that she couldn't think of just one.

The demons she wrestled with nearly every night.

Her family.

Her past.

Mercy.

But she settled on what she and Xóchitl could agree on. "I'm not as nice as you think," she said.

Xóchitl stepped closer until her every exhale brushed Mai's cheek. "What if I say I'll take you however you are?"

Mai smiled sadly and shook her head, because despite the best of intentions, no one ever accepted her for who she was.

CHAPTER 8

IT WAS A BEAUTIFUL DAY to take off from work. One of those typical Atlanta autumn days that made Mai happy she'd never accepted the teaching job in New York City, despite her longing to escape the Redstone name. With what she thought was pretty damn impressive willpower, Mai was consciously *not* thinking about Xóchitl and their talk after class, about how things had been left unresolved between then—a throbbing wound that Mai worried at when her mind had too little to do.

Like now, apparently.

Get it together, dammit.

Okay.

She took a deep breath and drew in the scent of the crisp fall air, smoky with crackling leaves and bright afternoon sun. Wearing black knee boots, designer jeans, and a see-through blouse that showed off one of her prettier bras, Mai tap-tapped down the sidewalk toward a popular Buckhead restaurant.

Mai knew she naturally walked like she was on the prowl. It was something one of her first lovers had told her—not that she moved through the world with confidence, which was what she wanted, but that she stalked through the world as if she was looking for the next thing to devour. It wasn't an impression she was proud of, because that was the way her mother moved. She'd seen it enough times to know.

So Mai changed. With each step, she altered herself just a little, shortening her stride, adding a dimple to her chin, straightening her back even more until the click of her heels against the sidewalk was the sound of an urgent businesswoman with limited time. Gradually, she changed the look of her clothes to a boring dark blouse, matching slacks, and high heels.

She lengthened her hair and pinched her features to something resembling stress. When she walked through the doors of the restaurant, she looked like someone else entirely, and when she saw the woman in the simple black dress at the hostess' station, she knew she'd found the right person.

Sunlight slanted through the wood and glass doors to splash the dark hardwood floors in gold. It was just after the desertion of the lunch crowd, and the entire restaurant felt like an exhale of relief.

"Good afternoon, Miss." The hostess greeted her with a professional but sweet smile. "Table for one?"

Mai nodded, and the hostess smiled even wider and led Mai to a table overlooking the back terrace, where she could stretch her legs out into the sun.

"A late lunch is the perfect thing," the hostess said, placing a menu in front of Mai. "You just missed the lunch crush." She lightly patted the menu. Clearly, she was a woman used to making things better for the people around her. "This table is a good one for the time of day. The sun is right here but not in your eyes, and you have a view of our garden from here without being out in the heat."

Mai would have preferred being completely in the heat, but she didn't say that.

"Your waitress will be with you shortly, but feel free to ask if I can help you in any way at all."

Mai nodded at her again, this time visibly relaxing her tight features and giving the woman the faintest of smiles. If possible, the hostess—and Mai knew her name was Tracy—perked up even more, the smile brightening and widening to show teeth so perfect they looked brand new.

"Thank you," Mai said and extended her legs into the promised patch of sun. Tracy turned away, still smiling, her entire body radiating satisfaction at a job done well.

Mai didn't have to look at the folder in her briefcase to remind herself how Tracy had looked nearly two years before. Surveillance stills from the local hospital she'd visited too often had captured a good view of her face, unmarked but purpled with a low-grade terror, as if the very oxygen inside her body had been strangled by fear.

In a moment of incredible strength, Tracy had gotten a rape kit done on one of these many hospital visits, but in the end, she withdrew the charges against her husband. After half a dozen more hospital visits, the husband caught the attention of the Absolution Killer. Although she'd been fairly certain before, Mai now knew without a doubt what linked the thirty-eight murders.

The folder she carried bulged with pictures and statements of people victimized by Absolution's targets. These people had been wrecked, torn apart, so someone else had taken away their pain.

Mai had verified the reason and the link between the victims. Now she just had to find the killer.

Cold shivered over her arms and down her back despite her sitting in the sun. No, she didn't want Absolution to get caught. But what choice did she have? It was either his life or hers, and she was still rather fond of living.

But that decision made and unmade itself during the hour it took her to get back to Poncey-Highlands and, because she didn't know what else to immediately do after the revelations from her visit to Buckhead, she wandered through the busy maze of streets in her neighborhood.

She'd taken the day off to visit the woman in Buckhead and do a few other things. Now that she'd finished what she'd set out to do, the day was free, hanging from her like a loose thread she wanted to yank away. Mai had never done well being idle.

A store was selling high-end clothing for what looked like poodles, and she spent much too long staring into the window and considering how a poodle would even get into a complicated-looking chartreuse sweater with too many buttons.

"Shopping for some new clothes?"

She turned at the sound of the amused voice and drew a sharp breath of surprise. The world had been moving as it wanted around her, humans threading through the late afternoon in their cars and on foot and in the air—in the constant hum of traffic and tapping footsteps on the sidewalk and the occasional cry of a siren that perked up her ears but not her attention. These things caught her notice and not the woman who moved up behind her. She would've made a terrible spy.

"Xóchitl." The woman took a bow as if Mai was introducing her onto a stage. "What are you doing here?"

Mai didn't know where the other woman lived, but she was fairly certain it was nowhere near Poncey-Highlands. For a wild moment, Mai thought Xóchitl had been following her. Then she dismissed the thought as ridiculous.

"Doing a bit of shopping," Xóchitl answered Mai's question, although her hands were empty.

Today she was wearing ankle boots, skinny jeans, and an off-the-shoulder gray blouse. On Xóchitl, the simple outfit made her look as if she'd just stepped off a fashion runway. She carried the same colorful messenger bag draped over her shoulder.

"Nothing strike your fancy yet?" Mai asked, gesturing to Xóchitl's empty hands.

"Oh, I'm just getting started."

They watched each other for a moment, the ghost of their last conversation swirling between them. Or at least that was how Mai felt, standing awkwardly in her dark clothes that were the complete opposite to Xóchitl, who burned brightly enough to light up the whole universe.

Oh God… Mai internally cringed at her thoughts, uncomfortably aware she was too far gone to save herself from infatuation.

A familiar ripple in the air and a rise of goose bumps on her skin jerked Mai's gaze over her shoulder in time to see Ethan appear on the sidewalk just behind her. He snarled at her, then immediately looked surprised to see Xóchitl. Mai startled when Xóchitl gripped her arm, but the other woman was looking at Ethan.

"Where did he come from?" Xóchitl asked, her voice low and calm.

"The gutter."

What was he doing there? Did her mother send him after her again?

Ethan settled on the busy street from wherever he'd just come from, looking around and then stroking the lapels of his navy suit as his expression smoothed into an approximation of a smile. The flash of teeth made Mai's skin crawl.

"I didn't know you had company," Ethan said. "I dropped by to chat with you about some family business."

She never had any business to discuss with him. "I'm sure whatever it is can wait." Mai gestured toward Xóchitl's oddly still form. "As you can see, I'm currently occupied."

"Maybe later on tonight, then?" he pressed.

"Maybe not."

Beside her, Xóchitl released a soft huff of breath that almost sounded like a laugh.

Ethan had the nerve to look angry. He bared his canines at her. "Playing hard to get, cousin?"

"You keep forgetting, Ethan," she said, "that I never play with you."

His look soured even more. He visibly bristled like an outraged cat, and Mai became aware that Xóchitl still had a hand wrapped around her wrist, a reminder that Mai could be doing more pleasant things than enduring her cousin's presence.

"Talk to Mother about whatever it is you need," she said, done with him and the unease he stirred along her skin. "You and I have nothing to discuss."

Mai wanted to turn her back to him then but didn't dare. Xóchitl didn't let go of her hand, and in the time it took for her to appreciate that fact all over again, Ethan disappeared. A few seconds later, Xóchitl's hand fell away.

"Well, that was an unpleasant person."

"You have *no* idea," Mai muttered, looking back at the empty space where her cousin had disappeared.

"It doesn't matter." Xóchitl shrugged like Ethan had never been there, then gestured to a restaurant half a block away. "Would you like to have lunch?"

But as easily as Xóchitl dismissed Ethan, it took a few moments for Mai to recalibrate her own attentions. She blew out a slow breath. "Ah…not really. I just had something to eat not too long ago."

"How about dessert, then?" Xóchitl stepped closer. Her vanilla, sun-warmed citrus perfume abruptly made Mai's mouth water. She could practically taste the flavors.

They were near one of Mai's favorite places, a French-style pastry shop and deli that served one of the best cakes she'd ever had the pleasure of putting in her mouth. They were also very near her condo.

Mai toyed with her earring, an uncharacteristically nervous gesture she stopped as soon as she realized she was doing it. "Dessert sounds like something I can do."

She ended up on her knees with the fur of Xóchitl's pussy scraping her lips. Mai muffled her cries of need in the hot flesh between Xóchitl's thighs, her hand stuffed down the unzipped front of her pants. Desire lit up her entire body, her orgasm pitifully close while Xóchitl tugged at her own bare nipples and writhed against the closed door of the condo.

"Fuck…that feels good." Xóchitl's hand fisted at the back of Mai's head, roughly guiding her mouth to the small space between her thighs that her jeans, only shoved down to her knees, allowed. "*You* feel—feel so good." A gasp broke through Xóchitl's words.

She was close, if her ragged gasps were anything to go by. And Mai was close too, Xóchitl's salty, slick clitoris calling for the slide of her tongue again and again as she moved her head in for more, thankful that the jeans had some form of spandex in them. She hummed her pleasure and stroked herself closer to the edge, unable to wait.

But she didn't have to wait, because soon Xóchitl was coming, groaning Mai's name and gushing her completion all over Mai's mouth, down her chin, and all over her blouse. That was all the permission Mai needed, and she curled fingers inside herself, the thumb on her clit stroking just so, until she was gasping into the hairs around Xóchitl's pussy, too far gone to do more than rub her face in the sticky, salty wet. Xóchitl's essence smeared all over her face, and Mai's entire body lit up with a shock blast of pleasure.

Breathless, she dropped her cheek against Xóchitl's thigh. When she was able to move again, she looked up the long, lean length of Xóchitl, at the untamed jungle of her pubic hair, her belly with its hint of roundness, the breasts bared by the sweater and bra pushed up to her neck and hanging down her back like a cape. Her skin was hot, nearly roasting under Mai's cheek.

This feels so perfect. So right.

Mai closed her eyes. This could really be nothing, she thought. Just sex. An illusion of compatibility. Only two women sating a mutual need. But Xóchitl's hand drifted to the back of Mai's head in a delicate caress, continuing down to her neck and following the curve of one ear with her thumb. Mai shuddered, weakening at the unfamiliar touch. It unerringly found the vulnerable places that turned her to jelly.

This is almost as good as the sex, Mai thought, dazed. Of all the things she'd never had but somehow missed, the biggest one was tenderness. The desire and willingness of a lover—of anyone—to comfort and soothe her.

She was in so much trouble with this woman.

Mai licked her lips, which had gone dry from her panting breaths. "So, do you think you know me better now?"

A smile took the corners of Xóchitl's mouth. "Not yet, but the day is still young." Thankfully, her hand stopped its lingering caress, and Mai could think again. But the hand disappeared from her ear, only to drag Mai to her feet. Xóchitl was surprisingly strong. "Show me your room," she said.

In Mai's bed, they fucked like it was going out of style, Xóchitl and her relentless fingers plunging deep inside Mai again and again to mine orgasm after orgasm from her body, barely letting Mai touch her again after that first time against the door. Only when Mai was tired, wrung out, and used up, her body smeared with fluids and the bed one giant wet spot, did Xóchitl push her onto her back and ride Mai's hip until her body shuddered with satisfied lust. Mai had stopped thinking after the fourth orgasm, her brains no doubt leaked from between her thighs to mingle with the other fluids on the sheets. She barely protested when Xóchitl lifted her in her arms again, shocking Mai with her easy strength, and gently placed her on the love seat to rummage through the linen closet for fresh sheets. Xóchitl changed them and tossed the sullied ones into the laundry hamper before reinstalling them both back in the bed.

Mai rolled her head lazily to the side and noticed with a far-off sense of surprise that it was nighttime. Outside the window, her little part of the city was enshrouded in darkness, the stars like pinpricks in the heavens. She had work in the morning and a visit to make to her mother's house. But the thought rolled through her mind, separate from any urgency. Thanks to the faint pulse beats of her satisfaction still throbbing between her thighs, she was as weak as a day-old kitten and more sated than she remembered being in a long time.

"How do you feel?" Xóchitl's breath whispered against the back of her neck, making Mai shiver.

She turned her head and sighed, overwhelmed by the warmth in solar-dark eyes close enough for her to drown in. Nothing in the last few months of knowing Xóchitl Bentley had led her to believe she'd ever get such a look from her.

"I'm great," Mai murmured, the words barely above a whisper. "Tired. You wore me out."

"That was the idea."

"Why?"

"Because you're too pent-up." Xóchitl drifted her fingers down the center of Mai's chest, a barely-there touch that comforted instead of aroused. "Your mind never shuts down. You never relax."

Mild alarm shivered up Mai's spine. "You don't know me that well."

"Not yet, but I'm beginning to." Xóchitl gave that almost-smile of hers again. "And I like what I know so far." Her fingers circled Mai's belly button, the touch like indistinct tongues of flame on her skin. A pleasure that hinted of more to come. "What are you always thinking so much about? Do these things keep you up at night?"

The questions gave Mai pause, pulling her from her lethargy with an unpleasant twist in her stomach. They were intimate, I'm-staying-longer-than-tonight questions. Not a good idea. The touch on Mai's belly disturbed her in a different way now. She squirmed against the sheets, wanting to move away, but not quite able to manage it.

Unwise work romance aside, it was dangerous for a human to come into her life. Her family would crush Xóchitl. Mai should push her away now, tell her to get out before they got any deeper into…whatever this was. But when Mai opened her mouth, honesty of a sort fell out.

"I think about my family," Mai said reluctantly. "I think about how things can go wrong." She flicked a look at Xóchitl's face and saw her looking back with complete attentiveness. Mai dipped her gaze away, falling into the reluctant memory of the first woman who'd looked at her that way. Her first girlfriend, a powerful Meta she'd known in boarding school. Someone outside the family who Mai had thought she could trust. The only thing she'd gotten from that relationship was more pain and proof that no Meta could be trusted with someone weaker than themselves. "The usual glass-half-empty thing. Nothing you want to hear about," Mai finished.

"Try me," Xóchitl said. She spread her palm flat over Mai's stomach, a proprietary gesture amplified by the glowing warmth in her eyes. "You might be surprised."

But Xóchitl's questions and Mai's memory of the girl who'd nearly broken her in boarding school turned her mind back toward other cruelties and the decision she'd made earlier that day to turn over all the information she found on Absolution to her mother.

The "mercy" her family would show Absolution wasn't one the killer deserved. No more than Mai had deserved the type of mercy her family and other Powerful Metas had shown her during her lifetime among them. Their mercy had nearly destroyed her. With the conscience she'd grown in the wild, could she throw Absolution to them? And if she could, did she deserve to have a woman like Xóchitl in her bed?

A low sound of alarm broke into the room, like an animal scenting a trap. Mai abruptly realized *she* had made that sound. Xóchitl's hand tightened on her belly.

"Are you okay?"

Mai shook her head. "No...I..." She sat up and pulled away from Xóchitl, the sheets rustling beneath her suddenly restless body. Uncertainty and the beginnings of fear turned her fingers cold. And she did what she'd always done in moments like these. She ran.

"I have to get ready for work tomorrow."

Xóchitl raised an eyebrow, smiling. "Is that my cue to go?" But there was worry in her eyes. "Because it's okay. I know I was being intrusive. It only makes sense for you to withdraw. My apologies."

Mai bit her tongue to stop her own apology. She'd been like this her entire adult life, a suspicious and guarded creature her family had created. It didn't make any sense to apologize for taking care of herself. She got out of bed and pulled on her robe. "I'll see you at school?"

"Of course." Xóchitl sat up in the bed, then parted her lips like she wanted to say something else. But in the end, she only shrugged and reached for her clothes.

She didn't make a production out of leaving and didn't try to hug Mai on her way out the door. She just touched her elbow, a caress that was oddly more intimate than any kiss.

"Get some rest," Xóchitl said and then was gone.

But when Mai went back to bed, rest would not come.

It was a rainy day when Mai walked up the main staircase of the house she never wanted to set foot in again. Her tread was quiet against the marble floors, though her key in the door had been warning enough to those inside that she was there. At this time of day, only the servants wandered the large house. Her mother was in her downtown Atlanta office, and her father was off doing one of his favorite things—escaping his wife.

Ethan was nowhere in sight, but after the stunt he pulled the day before, she wouldn't have been surprised if he suddenly showed up. She needed to get what she came for and leave. Quickly.

After her only class of the day, Mai had left the university campus, thankful that none of her students signed up for office hours. And even more thankful she didn't see Xóchitl again. Mai wanted her too much. Even more now that she'd had a taste. The woman was a temptation and a distraction she couldn't afford to indulge in.

She adjusted the dark-green leather jacket over her shoulders and kept going. Her palms were damp and clammy from learned fear, but she curled her fingers into her jacket pockets and walked steadily down the brightly lit hallway toward Stephen's office. Despite his fucked-up extracurricular activities, he'd chosen to live in the same house as his big sister and her family, maintaining only a small cabin in upstate New York as a lair.

The doorknob to his office moved easily beneath her hand, a cool, golden latch on the old-fashioned French doors. The frosted-glass doors gave a false impression of transparency. Mai breathed in the scent of antique wood and furniture polish and leaned back against the closed door, lashes fluttering but her heart as steady as she could make it without being dead. The office was just like she remembered.

An instant of mad panic scuttled under her chest, and she tightened her hand around the door handle at her back. The office was empty. It was just her. Not even his ghost lingered there. Another breath and she moved forward to the desk. She stood in the quiet for a moment longer, looking over the wide expanse of the neatly organized workspace without touching anything. She needed to be strategic and not rifle through it like a common thief, especially since what she was looking for wasn't particularly common.

Her eyes flitted around the room.

The desk and its five drawers. A wooden file cabinet. A painting on the wall that concealed a safe the whole family knew about. His computer, dark and quiet, on top of the desk. Those were the places she needed to search.

Okay.

Mai pulled a flash drive from her pocket and sat down at the desk to see what she could find. She booted up the computer, waited past the Windows logo, then dove in as soon as the wallpaper came up, her eyes skimming quickly across the image: a wide shot of a dock at sunset, two silhouetted figures sitting at the edge of the water, their legs dangling. One figure was short and slender, the other was twice its size, looming and spindly as an oak in winter. She knew that dock. She knew the nearby cabin.

It was only a quick glance, but it was enough to twist Mai's stomach.

You don't have time for this.

She didn't have the luxury of tripping down memory lane with the ghost of her dead uncle looming over her shoulder.

Fingers quick on the keyboard and mouse, she cloned the computer, sending the copy directly to the machine sitting on her desk across town. Then, just to satisfy her paranoid heart, she copied every Word and Excel file she ran across and saved them to a flash drive. While the drive finished copying, she looked through the drawers, the desk, the cabinet, being careful to put everything back where she found it, ultimately finding nothing until all that was left was the wall safe.

She stood in front of it, a fist clenched at her side. If the safe was empty, then this was it. She'd have nowhere else to search unless she went to the cabin in New York. Her stomach turned to lead at the thought of setting foot in that cabin again.

"Are you sure she came this way?"

Mai cursed. Her sister, Abi. And she didn't sound far enough away.

She fumbled with the heavy painting, almost dropping it on her foot. With another soft curse, she took a breath, then forced steadiness into her fingers hovering over the safe's combination lock.

Outside the door and down the hall, she could hear her sister talking again, probably to one of the maids who must've seen Mai pass through the house. She should have known her unexpected appearance would raise a flag or two. Just not so soon. A quick glance at her watch told her she'd barely been in the house ten minutes.

Behind her, the computer screen flashed with a dialogue box telling her the download was complete. She grabbed the flash drive and shoved it deep into her jeans pocket.

Back at the wall safe, with the clock ticking away the last of her private time with the combination lock, she extended her fingers again, trusting her instincts, spinning the combination for the numbers she knew were important to her uncle, the birthdate of her cousin, the child his human wife never allowed to live with him no matter how much the family threatened her.

03 18 01.

But the safe remained firmly locked.

Down the hall, the conversation between Abi and the maid was wrapping up. And her sister's footsteps began a purposeful tap toward where Mai warred with the memory of her uncle. *Fuck.* She'd been so sure that was it.

Then she remembered how he preferred to write out dates.

03 18 20 01.

A breath hissed from her throat when the lock released with a click. But she didn't waste time celebrating her success, only shoved aside what she wasn't looking for—half a dozen bricks of cash, a large baggie of coke, a few jewelry boxes—to scan over contracts, photos, anything else he thought worth safeguarding. Her hand shoved aside yet another jewelry box—there were over a dozen of them—when the box rattled in a way it shouldn't have. Mai frowned. She grabbed the box and flipped it open.

Instead of diamonds or rubies, the large ring box was neatly filled with flash drives, one tiny red drive slotted into each space where a ring would be.

Another breath. A hesitation. The sound of quiet footsteps heading down the hallway.

Making a quick decision, she flipped open all the boxes. Every one of them held flash drives. She grabbed a drive from each box and shoved the stolen drives into the inside pocket of her jacket, snapped the boxes closed, and stacked them the way she'd found them, then used her cell phone to snap photos of the pictures he'd kept in the safe. She slid everything back into place, clicked the safe door closed, and rehung the picture.

"What are you doing in here?"

Mai didn't flinch. She calmly turned from the painting, a portrait of her uncle and her mother as children. It was a copy of a photograph taken on the front porch of the house they'd been brought up in. Two children laughing, their eyes twinkling in conspiracy as they looked at each other in what Mai assumed was a candid moment. It was one of the few times she'd seen her mother really smiling.

"Hey, Abi." Mai sauntered away from the painting and gave her sister the most casual of glances before walking to the balcony of her uncle's study. "I heard about Uncle Stephen's death."

"Yes, we all did. The funeral is on Wednesday." Her sister walked further into the study but didn't close the door behind her. "You're probably glad he's dead, anyway."

Mai shrugged, not denying it. "It feels strange that he won't be in this place anymore. So unreal."

Such a relief. She stepped outside into the wet morning. The smell and sound of the rain helped to calm the remnants of Mai's nerves. She drew in a deep lungful of the fresh air.

"Are you coming to the funeral?" Abi asked.

"No." Mai had never been a hypocrite. Although she never talked with her sister about her feelings for Stephen Redstone, she'd never hidden them.

"I didn't think so. Just thought I'd ask." Abi shrugged, and the already precariously perched sleeve of her blouse fell off one shoulder.

She wore one of her typical hippie outfits, an oversized crocheted blouse and jean shorts, today complete with a crown of flowers braided through her thick hair. Although she was twenty-two and recently graduated from a Swiss university, she looked all of sixteen. She was a self-proclaimed sophisticate who'd spent most of her life away at boarding school, something their father had insisted on. She was both better and worse off for it.

"I thought you were heading back to Switzerland." Mai leaned over the railing, looking down onto the waters of their Olympic-sized pool, rippling from the steady patter of raindrops. She briefly wondered if anyone swam in the pool anymore.

"I am, but not until after the funeral." Like a good daughter, Abi had come back to Atlanta for the Conclave. Their mother must have found out about Stephen's death within hours of it happening and asked Abi to stay for the funeral too. Mandaia knew better than to ask Mai to come. If she came anywhere near that funeral, she'd probably set fire to the casket and all the hypocrites there.

"I still don't get why you hate him so much, Mai," Abi said. "He was our uncle." The concern in her sister's voice was sweet, but it made Mai choke. Stephen didn't deserve any sweetness in death, just as he hadn't deserved any in life.

Mai winced around her smile. "I'm glad you don't understand, Abi. I really am."

Her sister stepped close enough to affectionately bump Mai's shoulder and offer a small smile. Only ten years separated them, but it might as well have been a hundred. Abi had power. She'd had the privilege of growing up away from home and getting the version of their mother the rest of the world saw, smiling and tender, the successful multibillionaire businesswoman and former talk show queen who was proud of her children and playfully chagrined at their choices not to pursue careers in any of the family businesses.

Abi didn't want to come back to America, and except for visits like this one, she didn't have to. She had a gorgeous European boyfriend, school friends who invited her skiing every winter, and a childhood kept relatively safe in the fortress of one of the best Swiss boarding schools for Meta children. Some days, Mai tried not to envy her.

"Sometimes I wish I felt more a part of this family," Abi said a few minutes into their loaded silence.

Mai looked at her sister in surprise, but Abi shrugged and turned her back to the railing and draped her arms along the rain-damp iron, her body an elegant line even in cutoffs. The chunky crystals on her long necklace rattled with her movement.

"It's true," Abi said. "You all have so many shared secrets I don't have a clue about. I see hints of those secrets in your faces and in the things you don't tell me, even now, when you talk about Uncle Stephen. There's something about him the whole family knows that no one will tell me." She shook her head, and the flower crown fluttered in the breeze along with the swaying cloud of her hair. "The version of the family I see when I come home for holidays doesn't feel like the real one." She looked at Mai with a slow blink. "And I think you know what I mean?"

"I do."

But how could Mai tell Abi that her version was the best one for her to know? She'd never considered that her sister might have felt like an outsider, only that she was protected from everything Mai had endured as a child. Abi's abilities had presented themselves spectacularly and suddenly. There had been no need to test her to find out what she could do and what her place would be in the family. She hadn't been drowned again and again by someone who was supposed to love her.

The memory of that afternoon under choking water never left Mai. But that memory wasn't something she wanted to saddle her young sister with. Abi had her escape. She had a better life away from all this. Still, her lightness and the kind glow in her eyes charmed Mai and made her want to get to know her only sister for real.

She turned to Abi. "Why don't you—"

"Coming to steal the china again, Mai?"

Her teeth snapped shut over the rest of what she was about to say. Abi jumped and looked toward the source of the voice, the doorway where Ethan stood. He must have teleported onto the grounds from wherever he was, then walked into the house like everyone else because of the protective power fields her mother put around the property.

Mai had been aware of footsteps at the back of her mind but had paid them little attention since she'd gotten what she came for. She glanced briefly over her shoulder at Ethan but said nothing to him. Mai still hadn't gotten over him just turning up the day before to supposedly discuss family business. It didn't make any sense.

"As the oldest, she'll inherit all this," Abi said. "Why would she have to steal anything when it already belongs to her?" Her tone implied that nothing in the house belonged to him. Mai allowed herself a small smile before she straightened and turned fully to face her cousin. He looked like he'd just swallowed a spoonful of dog shit.

"Your mother sent me when she heard you were here," he said.

"Well, to save you and her any further panic, I'll just head out."

As Mai walked past him, he looked her over as if he could see through her clothes to what she carried in her pockets. Normally, he wouldn't hesitate to push into Mai's personal space and interrogate her. Strangely, he was reluctant to engage in his usual bullshit with Abi around.

"Will I see you before I leave, Mai?" her sister asked, although she kept her frowning gaze on Ethan. "I want to talk more about what I was saying before."

Mai's suspicion reared its head, but she consciously restrained it.

"Sure. I can drop by and pick you up after the funeral." All of her shuddered with revulsion at the thought of coming back to the house with her mother in it, though. At her sister's knowing look, she thankfully changed direction. "Or you can stop by my place."

"Okay. I'll text you when I'm on the way."

"Cool. See you then."

Ethan's power meant he could travel just about anywhere he wanted within the blink of an eye; he could even grab Mai and teleport her somewhere she didn't want to be. As if that didn't worry her in the least, she sauntered past him. As she did, Abi stepped toward their cousin and asked a question, low voiced but urgent sounding, giving Mai the perfect chance to damn near run from the house, never more grateful that it was impossible for her cousin to teleport into a moving vehicle.

Her condo had nearly the same protections as her mother's house, and so far, they had proven strong enough that only her mother had been able to get past them. As she sped through the early afternoon traffic, she hoped that still held true.

At home, she reinforced the protective fields around the condo and immediately went into her office, flash drives in hand, to the computer. Her mother wanted her to find out what happened to Stephen, but it was interesting *and* telling that Mandaia didn't offer any information about what her uncle had been doing that attracted a killer like Absolution.

She settled in front of her computer and turned on the machine, listening the whole while for any noises that did not belong. So far, there was nothing but the faint hum of the fridge, the heater set on low despite the already warm weather, and the creak of the leather chair under her.

The clone of Stephen's computer sat next to hers, but right now she was more interested in the things he'd kept hidden, the small flash drives in the ring box and the photos she'd taken.

Mai clicked on the first drive, holding her breath, then released a relieved sigh when all that came up were numbers on a spreadsheet. She'd been anticipating the worst. Then she began to look carefully at them. Her relief ended.

Even though the drives had been hidden, the information itself wasn't even encoded. The digital trail on the first of the small devices was practically a red carpet rolled out through the glaring and suspicious debits from her uncle's main accounts.

And with each revelation, she couldn't stop thinking about Ethan and how he just kept showing up. Mai frowned at the computer, unable to shake a nagging feeling.

With the cloned hard drive open to her uncle's calendar, she easily matched the dates of her uncle's "fishing trips" he took twice a year to a payout, usually in the thousands. The GPS history from his phone that she accessed remotely allowed her to trace his movements, the money, the victims. It shouldn't have been that easy to find, but it was.

Based on where her uncle had been, how much money was paid out, the headlines of missing children, and the hospital records she looked through until her eyes burned, he had been the cause of at least one suicide.

A girl killed herself because of him. *Killed herself.*

Her fingers went ice cold while the details of the young girl's death stared back at her in stark black and white from the computer screen.

She could have been like this poor girl. Broken. Driven mad by a man who cared more for his own sick pleasure than preserving the childhood and lives of girls who came in contact with him.

Who's to say you're not mad now? A reedy voice whispered at the back of her mind.

Despite her horror at each thing she found, Mai kept looking. Her mother had taught her a long time ago—one of the few positive lessons Mandaia had passed on to her—that humans were frail and shouldn't be broken. Metas needed them as much as they'd been trained to need us. Breaking them would serve no purpose. But that apparently wasn't a lesson she'd passed on to Stephen.

He'd broken enough humans and other vulnerable people that someone had emerged from the ether to break *him* in return. And Mai couldn't help but feel a hot burn of satisfaction for it.

Something inside her wished she'd been there to see it.

To watch the blade carve into his skin again and again.

To trap a leather-covered palm over his mouth when he tried to scream.

To strip every dignity from him, piece by piece, violation by violation, breath by breath.

Mai shook herself from her blood-smeared fantasies. It didn't do her any good to wish those things. She had enough to occupy her now. Refocused, she dove into the files again, looking not just at her uncle but at the children he victimized and their would-be protectors, the people who were around them and realized too late what needed to be done to keep them safe. Unlike the police, she expanded her search beyond American borders until she found similar cases in Canada and what seemed like the very first Absolution killing in Mexico.

She frowned at the obscure news article she found, buried as an anecdote in an American tourist's blog.

Interesting.

A pattern emerged slowly, a thread. And she tugged on it, turned it over, peered at it from every angle until the truth was too bright to ignore. The leather creaked as Mai sat back.

The first Absolution kill she found was a man in his fifties. Mai traced a connection between him and a young woman, a freshman in college, who'd drowned under suspicious circumstances. The girl had a surviving brother, but he was very much a human. Every sign pointed to him being the Absolution Killer, yet how could a human, even one swollen with grief, bring down a beast like Stephen Redstone?

Mai was missing something, something she was very close to finding.

But what is it?

She sighed in frustration, running her hands over her thick hair and down to the back of her neck. Her head hung low. It was late, nearly two in the morning according to her phone.

Maybe fresh eyes could help her see what was just on the edge of her awareness. Fighting a yawn, she stood up and stretched. Her back cracked, each vertebrae making a sound like slowly popping corn. She groaned from the hint of pain there.

I've definitely been at it too long, she thought. Even her body was telling her she needed a break.

Mai closed the computer and stood up, but something made her pause. She ejected the flash drive and, along with the others she'd gotten from Stephen's safe, tucked it in a hidden closet drawer. Just in case. She knew well enough that her mother had no boundaries.

Then, without bothering with her usual shower, she fell into bed naked, the thin covers pulled up over her ears.

The light is wrong. Sunset and sunrise are both happening at the same time, brightness coming at Mai from both sides of the long porch. Usually, she loves the light, but this brightness makes her flinch, and when she huddles down to protect herself against it, her shoulders tucking up around her ears, she realizes she is a child. The breath hesitates in her throat.

She is powerless and vulnerable, sitting in a chair too big for her small bones, too high for her short legs. The light comes from both sides, but instead of burning, it is cold. She shivers and curls even more into the chair, tucking her feet under herself and cowering back. She feels a presence rising from the direction of the sunrise, but whoever it is, she can't see them, only their silhouette, tall and vaguely female, approaching her on quiet feet.

"Who is it?" Her childish voice quavers.

But whoever it is says nothing, and Mai is left to stare into the blinding sun, eyes squinting uselessly against the glare. The person comes closer, and she stares harder. Just when she thinks she can make out their features, a heavy hand lands on her shoulder from behind, from the direction of the sunset. Too late, she hears the heavy boot steps. Surprised air rises up in her throat to choke her, and before she can turn around, a plate of cookies lands in her lap. She jumps, and the cookies tumble off the white plate, off her lap, and to the ground.

The sunset feet come closer, and the crunch of cookies under heavy shoes is loud on the otherwise quiet porch. The suns hover, neither rising nor falling, just burning Mai with their united cold fire until she thinks she will die from the shivers that wrack her body.

From the direction of sunset, a glass of milk appears under her nose, and she turns her head away. She hates milk. But the owner of the boot steps, also hidden in silhouette, keeps pushing the milk toward her, putting it to her mouth, choking her with it until she is crying and the milk is running down her chin and she is dying, dying, dying. And screaming out for—

Mai sat up in bed with a gasp, clawing at her own throat, the sound of her labored breathing a loud and wet rattle in the bedroom.

"Bad dream?"

A masked woman sat on the edge of her sheets, one leg drawn up to rest comfortably against the mattress, the other on the floor. She wore an outfit Mai would have worn once upon a time. Black and skintight. An expensive type of jumpsuit, the material snug enough to show off her shape. Soft leather boots brushed just below her knees. She wore matching leather gloves. A leather jacket sat unzipped over the slender torso. A mask covered her entire face and head. Even her eyes were hidden, concealed by dark, green-tinted goggles that looked heavy-duty enough for night vision.

Swimming from the terror of her dream, Mai was more afraid of what she was running away from than what was in front of her. "Get out."

"You're not very welcoming, are you?"

The voice was deep but feminine. Even muffled under the mask, something about its low, mocking quality rang a faint but familiar bell at the back of Mai's mind. But she wasn't in the mood to pursue it.

"Don't make me repeat myself," Mai said.

The sheet had fallen down around her hips, baring her breasts and stomach to the woman, but she refused to pull it back up. She was sick of people breaking into her apartment and trying to make her uncomfortable in the place she lived.

The woman sighed and moved. At first, Mai thought she was getting up, but she only leaned back in the bed, balancing her weight on her flattened palms and settling that glowing green gaze on Mai.

"I'll make this quick since you're feeling so inhospitable."

"I'd rather you just leave," Mai snapped.

The woman tilted her head, a coy movement that reminded Mai of a cat, absolutely relaxed, absolutely amused. "Wouldn't you be even the slightest bit disappointed if I left without telling you why I went through the trouble of breaking into your very secure little place?"

"No, not at all."

"Liar." Laughter rang in her voice. "Liar, Liar. Mercy on fire."

"How did you—?" Mai started to get up, her heart tripping faster in her chest.

Suddenly the woman wasn't idle anymore. "No. I'd rather you stay there, if you don't mind." Her lean figure was all readiness and corded muscle underneath the thin suit and jacket.

Mai slid her feet from under the covers anyway. The woman was on top of her in a heartbeat, smelling of exhaust and leather. Her weight easily pinned Mai to the bed while her hands clasped Mai's wrists and held them down. One of the things Mai prided herself on was her speed. She might not be as strong as others in the family, but she moved fast enough that she didn't have to be. This woman made her feel like she was moving through sludge. She'd only just thought of leaping across the small expanse before she was held down and gasping under the slight but immovable weight.

"I don't want to hurt you," the woman said. Her breath whispered against Mai's cheek through the face mask.

"Then leave." *And don't tell anyone about Mercy.*

"I can't. Not yet." She shifted slightly on top of Mai, getting a tighter grip on Mai's wrists. The leather jacket brushed over the skin of Mai's breasts and then her nipples, and she shuddered inexplicably at the contact.

"This investigation you're doing," the woman continued, "you have to stop."

Not this again.

Mai ground her teeth in annoyance and anger. First the cops, then her family, and now this stranger. Her uncle was proving to be as much trouble in death as he'd been in life.

"And what if I don't stop? Are you going to break my legs? Tell the people I work for something about me they shouldn't know?" She bucked in the woman's grip, growling. But the woman didn't move a single inch.

"No," the woman said, her voice going softer than before. "If you don't stop, you'll discover something even more dangerous." Her breath brushed against Mai's cheek again.

"Dangerous for who?"

"For you"—Mai didn't even try to smother her incredulous laugh—"and for me."

Mai went absolutely still. Her heart began a hard beat in her chest, a frantic rhythm that even finding a dangerous stranger in her bed hadn't initiated. "Was it you?" she asked. "Are you the one who killed him—them?"

The woman shifted on top of her, the cool zipper on her leather jacket rasping again over Mai's bare breasts and belly. "Does it matter?" The hands around her wrists tightened briefly, grinding the bones together. But it seemed like a reflex, not a deliberate cruelty. "He wasn't a good person. None of them were."

"But you don't get to say who is good or bad, and you sure as hell don't get to decide who dies."

"I do a lot of things without permission, Mandaia-Pili."

Mai bristled, not missing that the woman knew who she was. Maybe even *what* she was. But she focused on the obvious and most annoying. "Don't call me that."

The woman sat back, still pinning Mai's legs with her weight. She sighed, and her breath moved over Mai's cheek, down to her throat. "The world is a complicated place. You can't escape where you came from any more than I can."

For a moment, the stranger was a quiet and thoughtful weight on top of Mai, her mind seemingly very far away. Then she shook, and through the mask, those eyes fixed on Mai again.

"Don't pursue this, Mai. It won't lead you anywhere good."

Then she was off the bed and slipping through the bedroom door Mai had closed before she went to sleep. Mai leaped up to follow but quickly lost sight of her. Seconds later, she heard the faint click of the living room window and ran toward it. She threw it open, fingers gripping the ledge as she stared out into the empty night.

The woman was gone.

Mai wasted seconds staring out the window before she remembered the work she'd been doing before bed. With a curse, she ran to the desk, banging her knee into the edge of the wooden antique in her haste to grab the computer and turn it on. The machine was hot, scorching under her fingers. She hissed in surprise but didn't take her hand off the power button. The machine didn't turn on. Mai tried again, frantically pressing then holding down the button. Sparks shot from the side of the computer. She jumped back just as a trail of smoke snaked from the keyboard.

Shit.

Anger and panic rising, she took stock of the conspicuously empty surface of her desk. Her cell phone was gone. All the files she'd been working on. The photos and notes from the police investigation. Everything was gone.

She cursed again, ready to run to the cupboard and check on the hidden flash drives, but forced herself to stand still in case the woman was still somewhere watching.

It won't lead you anywhere good. The woman's words rang like warning bells in Mai's ears.

But as far as she was concerned, Stephen Redstone was the one leading her down this path, not anything or anyone else. He'd forged this path years ago, long before the first victim died under the blade of the Absolution Killer. Long before Mercy saved her first human. She could no more stop her search now than she could stop herself from breathing.

CHAPTER 9

MAI COULDN'T GO BACK TO sleep. Worried that someone was watching her, she left the ruined computer and locked herself in her bedroom, took a quick and cool shower to shock her system, then got dressed. In her car, she drove to the nearest 24-hour-discount-everything shop, bought a laptop, and took it to an all-night coffee shop along with the flash drives.

By the time the sun came up, she'd found more than enough.

Mai rubbed the exhaustion from her eyes and stared into space while the coffee shop woke up around her. The mystery woman was right. This wasn't the road she wanted to be on. It led only to the darkest places and made her wish she'd never started on the journey. But she couldn't turn back now.

At 9:15 a.m., she was at her mother's office, armored in her black leather jacket, jeans, and long boots. With her files.

"Is she in?" She stood in front of her mother's secretary with her hands in her pockets, her look deliberately casual.

"Unfortunately, no." Eldridge, the man who'd been with Mandaia for as long as Mai had been visiting the office, gave her a brief but friendly smile. "Your brother is here, though. He told me to show you into his office if you came by."

Mai frowned. The last time she saw Cayman, he didn't seem in any hurry to talk with her, any more than she was to talk with him, other than to initiate the usual set of torments, anyway.

"All right." She dropped her files on Eldridge's desk. "Just make sure she gets these in case she comes in the next few minutes. Tell her to read them carefully."

"Of course." He was already putting a sticky note on the manila folder, simultaneously getting up to walk toward Mandaia's office, when Mai turned in the opposite direction toward her brother's office.

At the door, she knocked once before trying the knob. But it was locked.

"I'm here, Cayman. What do you want?"

When the lock clicked open, she went in. Her brother, dressed surprisingly in jeans and a sweater—a casual look he didn't normally go for in the office—was walking back to the desk. She closed the door behind her.

"What's going on?"

He leaned back against his desk, arms crossed. "I hear you were stirring up trouble." The look he leveled on her was vaguely paternalistic, and it immediately raised Mai's hackles.

"I haven't been doing anything but minding my own business," she said. "Can you say the same?"

"This family is my business, and I'm taking damn good care of it, unlike you." A cascade of wrinkles formed on her brother's brow. "You're the one *not* taking care of us the way you should, running around with the humans and pretending to be one of them."

Running around with humans? Where was he getting his information from? Her mind briefly fell to Xóchitl, and the thought of Cayman spying on her, on *them*, made her vision go white with anger. "What the fuck are you up to, boy?"

"I may be younger than you, but I'm no boy." His teeth audibly clicked shut after the last word.

Mai ignored him, too far gone to care about his *feelings*. "If this is the conversation you wanted to have, you can have it by yourself. I have more important things to deal with."

He stepped toward her, his posture threatening. "Like what? Betraying Uncle Stephen and protecting his killer from us?"

Protecting his killer? Because she was working with the enforcers?

Although Mai knew what Cayman was capable of, her mind stuttered. Her little brother was stalking toward her, fists at his sides as if he wanted to attack her. "What the actual fuck…?" She braced herself—feet wide, her own fists raised.

"You didn't think I knew about that, did you?" Cayman stopped barely two feet away. "It's obvious you don't want to be part of this family anymore, but I never thought you'd betray us like this."

Heat washed through Mai, the most dangerous and incinerating kind. Her reason flew past the gates she'd held tight for far too long.

"You don't get to lecture me about betrayal!" she snarled. The warm air of the office washed over her bared teeth. "Not *ever*." Not after the way he abandoned her, along with the rest of the family, when she was a child. "Do you even know what you're protecting?" She didn't wait for him to answer. "Did you know Stephen raped little girls and got away with it for years, thanks to our mother?" The thumb drives she'd found in the safe, the photos, even the financial records painted a picture of complicity that made her sick.

Cayman's eyes narrowed. If Mai didn't know any better, she'd say her brother looked…surprised. But if Mandaia knew everything and covered for Stephen, it only made sense that Cayman did too. Wasn't this the information he protected so rabidly?

But the surprise quickly cleared from his face, replaced by suspicion. Denial. "That's bullshit, and you know it." He sneered at her. "You *are* trying to destroy the family from the inside, making up these crazy stories about Uncle Stephen and our mother. Ethan was right."

"Ethan…? What—?"

The air rippled around them, an unpleasant sensation that only meant one thing. Mai spun to put her back to the door and get ready for Ethan, but before she could move again, rough hands grabbed her shoulders and yanked her backward. Her brother's office wavered in front of her eyes, then disappeared, its luxurious confines replaced by a place Mai remembered all too well.

"No!" She nearly screamed in panic.

Her body shivered with the shock of it. Her mind reeled from the spiked memories of one long afternoon trapped in this place. But even with the disorientation, her body readied to take advantage of the small moment of *settling* that happened once they solidified in the new location. She wasn't a helpless child anymore.

Mai shoved away from Ethan, tumbling away from him in a somersault before he could get his bearings. Immediately, she sensed the presence of others in the room, two men, as she turned in the air. She landed in a crouch.

Cement floor. Soundproof walls. A warehouse in the middle of nowhere with roaring freight trains regularly moving past. In the center of the room, there was a tall and wide water tank that looked big enough to house a school of sharks. A scream of terror rattled inside her head, ready to be set free, but she clamped her mouth shut.

Just as when she was a child, there would be no one here to help her.

The two men rushed her, both of them massive, and their hands gripped tight onto her arms through the leather jacket. Then she felt Ethan's presence in a wavering of space too close to her, a fist solidifying before her eyes before it slammed into her face with the sound of worlds exploding. The pain shattered her.

Her body crashed into the cement floor. Hot, red blood gushed from her nose, down to her mouth and chin. Her vision swam. Ethan's grinning face appeared above Mai as he fully materialized, his solid figure in another one of his damn designer suits.

"Stupid bitch." He laughed. "You'll never see me coming."

Darkness swarmed over Mai and dragged her down.

When Mai surfaced again, she was hanging upside down above the water tank.

The air rushed into her lungs on a gasp of panic. Below her, the clear water rippled faintly, deep enough to drown her a hundred times over. Her head felt heavy, her body weak and thick with pain. Her hands were zip-tied behind her back, tight enough to cut into her skin.

Chains rattled. She looked up and saw her ankles were also zip-tied together, but a chain was looped around her legs and draped over an industrial-sized hook hanging from the ceiling. She flopped from it like a fish. Fucking catch of the day.

A drop of blood slid down her face and fell into the water.

"Oh, good." Her cousin's voice. "Sleeping Beauty awakes."

Ethan was below and behind her, out of sight, but she felt him as strongly as the enhanced plastic ties around her wrists. His two lackeys stood at different points in the room, both of them watching her. They had ripped the jacket off her body, leaving her in the thin shirt and jeans she'd been taken in.

The water below Mai was as still and deep as death. This was the same tank they'd used on her when she was twelve. Terror roared toward her, its jaws wide enough to swallow her whole. Her breath rattled in her chest. Cold sweat rushed over her skin under her clothes.

No. Not again.

The chains around her feet and knees rattled again as she thrashed back and forth on the hook. She tried to reach up and free her feet, but her stomach muscles burned with the effort. Her body was too weak. Mai stopped trying and sagged from the hook.

She was afraid. Shit, she was terrified.

"I didn't want you to miss the second best part of this whole thing." Her cousin chuckled as he came into view, his suit impeccable, only his habitual pocket square missing. He looked like he was heading out for a stroll in the park, not about to start torturing his cousin to death.

But then he bared his teeth in a shark's grin.

Fuck.

She remembered that look all too well. Spurred headlong into a newer, deeper fear, Mai thrashed and whimpered low in her throat, trying again uselessly to buck herself off the thick hook that held her above the water.

"That's it," he crooned with a smile. "That's the desperation I want to see."

He dragged a wheeled platform close to the tank. Three steps up the platform brought him closer, and he grabbed a solid-looking device, a remote control of some sort from the topmost step of the platform, and pushed it. A harsh electrical noise sounded, and the chains holding Mai up shuddered. The wires attached to the hook whirred and lowered her closer to the water.

No! Mai thought she screamed it but wasn't sure. The breath stormed in her throat, and tears of fear burned her eyelids. Behind Ethan and out of sight, she twisted her wrists in the zip-ties.

"Are you going to beg me now?" Her cousin looked more than pleased at the thought. But Mai locked her jaws tight. He shrugged. "Too bad."

He dropped her into the water.

Mai had enough time to pull in a deeper breath. But memories of the past wrenched her mouth open into a scream. Water rushed in, a clean current of death that took her back, back, back to being a frightened twelve-year-old with too little power. A twelve-year-old who was begging to be released but instead was underwater with her wrists bound together in front and her ankles tied. Water had gushed into her mouth with each scream, the water expanding her chest, choking her, while her mother and uncle had watched and waited from the dry side of the tank for her to save herself.

But she'd been dying, even as outside the tank, her mother stood with fluttering fingers near her lips, chanting quietly something that Mai had only recognized in this revisited nightmare.

Change, her mother had quietly mouthed. *Change. Reach for your power. Take it. Don't let this be the end for you.*

But Mai hadn't changed. She couldn't have. She hadn't had the strength. Her power had only been enough for her to shift her face into the most pitiful look it could give, surface alterations that did nothing to save her and that had only earned Mandaia's pity once they'd dragged her out of the tank and left her gasping like a landed fish on the cold, hard ground.

Twenty years later, even the cold burn of her mother's pity was nowhere to be found.

Mai's body jerked with pain as her legs were yanked up and back. She was being moved through the water and above it. Mai gagged and coughed, her throat burning as the water sluiced off her.

"That was just for fun." Ethan grinned while she gasped and twisted above the tank with water dripping down her face, cool as death against her skin. He stood with an electric cattle prod in both hands, jabbing it in the air as if he were sparring with an invisible opponent. "This is where the fun ends," he said, "for you."

He hefted the cattle prod high so Mai couldn't have ignored it if she wanted to. Dread gripped her throat. "Now, let's get started, shall we?" The corners of his eyes crinkled with false humor. "Tell me, Mai. Who is the Absolution Killer?" His voice was almost gentle. "Tell me the name of the bastard who killed my father."

CHAPTER 10

M AI REMEMBERED THAT DAY SHE lost everything. She'd walked toward home from school, twelve years old and excited about the field trip to the Georgia State Capitol Building to see what options she had as a Meta for the future. On the way home, she found a kitten, a sweet and nearly blind tabby she'd sheltered in the open front pocket of her backpack. The kitten's squeaking meows were so adorable she wanted to show it to her mother right away. She wanted to keep it.

The house was full of people when she slammed the heavy front door shut. Voices came from upstairs where her mother talked with one of the servants about dinner plans while her brother watched it all from the main staircase, idly levitating the marbles their mother had given him to help strengthen his power.

Although he was two years younger than Mai, his power had already shown itself and was already strong. Mai knew her mother worried she'd never manifest more than the parlor trick of being able to change her appearance at will.

"What's going on?" she'd asked Cayman, who waved at her from the middle of the stairs.

Her brother only shrugged. "They're talking about you today. It doesn't sound good." He looked at the squirming shape at the front of her school bag. "Hey, what's that?"

"A kitten. I found her on the way home. You want to see?"

Her brother's enthusiasm made her forget his earlier words. With a new kitten to care for and a field trip the next day, what was there for her to worry about?

Cayman clambered down the stairs to touch her kitten and laugh at its helplessness. But his hands on the little thing she'd already named Emmie, after her glowing emerald eyes, were gentle.

"Do you think Mom will let me keep her?"

"I doubt it." He scratched the kitten's head and was rewarded with a burst of squeaks. They both grinned. "But maybe she'll ask one of the maids to keep it, and then you can see it anytime you want."

His optimism made her hopeful too, and it was with that hope warming her chest that she looked up when her mother appeared with one of the family lawyers and with a man and a woman Mai didn't know.

"We have a test for you, Mai," her mother said.

Mai remembered being annoyed. She didn't want to take a stupid test. She wanted to play with Emmie and maybe get a snack. But she'd never been a rude child, so she just asked, "What test?"

Then her entire world as she knew it had drowned, never to resurface again.

Much later, as they had crouched over her soaked, gasping body on the cement floor, one of the strangers, the woman, took a stethoscope out of her bag and watched Mai with eyes filled to the brim with pity.

The first touch of the electric cattle prod tore Mai's throat wide open. Her screams rattled everything around her. The burn of electricity seared into her bare neck, into her skin for so long, she thought her scream, the agony, would never end.

She panted in the aftermath, staring at her cousin with eyes that felt as wide as the moon.

Ethan chuckled. "While that was pretty, it wasn't exactly what I'm waiting to hear." He cocked his ear toward her in a parody of listening. "Who." He pushed the prod into her shoulder. "Killed." Her chest. "My." Her belly. "Father?" Her jaw.

He held the cattle prod there the longest, through the wail of her screams. Her body jerked with the force of the electric current, and her insides crackled and burned, rolling flash fires of pain.

"I'm—not telling you shit!"

But while her mouth said what she should, her mind was jittering on the edge, waiting to babble the information, since it had a suspicion what Ethan would do next. The pain was nothing. Hanging upside down like a sacrificial sardine was nothing. It was the water—hovering just beneath her and waiting again to take her breath away—that rippled fear through her like a shock wave.

The terror burned through her lungs. But this was nothing compared to what they would do to Absolution once they got their hands on him.

"Fuck off," she huffed toward her cousin.

He dropped her back into the water.

Her entire body shuddered as it splashed into the tank. She twisted under the water, the chains around her feet rattling in her ears as they released from the hook, and she sank fast with nothing to hold her up. This time, she held her breath, knowing she couldn't last long underwater without the chains ready to drag her back to the surface.

Oh God. Oh God. Oh God.

Through her alternately dimming and sharpening senses, Mai knew her cousin condemned her with his cold eyes while the others in the room watched her with a little more concern. One of the men guarding the door came closer, gesturing wildly to her, trying to get her cousin's attention, but Ethan's eyes focused only on her. She knew she was dying. Not just from the water, but from the panic flooding her body. Frantic, she pulled at the ties behind her back, but the cuffs were strong and she was weak, so damn weak.

"You're nothing!" Ethan shouted at her through the glass, his face pressing close enough that his nose touched the tank. His eyes burned with madness. "You, the weak humans, and those pieces of meat who didn't deserve to be called Meta." Spit flew from his mouth and flecked the glass. "You're not a real Meta. You're not even a real Redstone. You should have protected him and our family, just like I did."

Protected him?

Mai twisted wildly to get close to the glass. She banged her head against it, her chest tight from holding her breath while she tried and tried to last until someone came to save her. *She* was the one who needed Mercy now.

She banged her head against the glass again, the pain and booming sound ricocheting through her, begging for someone to do something.

No matter what he said, Ethan didn't want her to talk. He wanted to shut her up. That much was obvious with each second Mai fought for breath. This wasn't about torturing her for information about the Absolution Killer, although he probably did want to know who it was so he could kill them. More than anything else, though, he wanted to kill her. And he soon would.

"She's dying!" one of Ethan's men shouted from very near the tank. Mai heard the words as clearly as if he had whispered them in her ear. "Mandaia didn't tell you to kill her."

"Get her out!" the other man called out. "The hook came loose."

"Her mother didn't want this!"

"Fuck Mandaia. This is between me and this bitch, no one else." Ethan stared at her, unblinking, and she silently—desperately—pleaded with him. With anyone.

I'm dying. The faint voice, which sounded too much like the twelve-year-old her, ramped up Mai's panic.

Terror blind, she bucked and jerked in the water, her breath leaking out in weak bubbles, even as she tried to hold it. A too-hot flame roared through her, forcing her mouth open wide to scream. Water rushed into her mouth.

Her pulse drummed in her ears. Her body burned. It felt like her insides were splitting open, her skin peeling off.

So fucking hot.

Mai slashed at the shirt over her chest. She'd broken free of the zip ties. She panted with relief, hands flying up to bang against the glass and beg again. Her fingers were spread wide against the glass and tipped with long nails that curved hard like talons. They scraped the glass with a sound like a scream.

She stared at her hands, then at the people gaping at her from outside the tank, their shocked faces a mirror of what she was feeling.

Her cousin gaped at her neck. Mai touched herself there and felt the slits. Gills. Mai panted, her mouth open.

Breathing. She was breathing.

Her body was light enough to maneuver in the water despite her ankles being tied together. But they didn't have to be. She bent double, slitting the zip ties with a fingernail. The superhardened plastic parted like paper.

Ethan stared at her with wide eyes. Mai stared back. And banged her fist against the glass. Fury destroyed her fear. She rattled the glass with her fist again, and the entire tank shook. That seemed to galvanize her cousin. With the cattle prod in hand, he surged toward her, and Mai shrieked with anger, tensing her body in preparation for the electric shock. But the current passed harmlessly through the water. Mai's jaws snapped together in surprise, and she felt her newly sharp teeth, the deadly and eel-like fluidity in her body.

She and Ethan realized at the same time what that meant. He jumped back, and she leapt up to the top of the tank, its smooth glass edges sliding under her scaled palms. In the air, she felt her body warming again, changing to compensate for the abundance of oxygen.

Mai landed on top of Ethan and latched onto him before he could take another step. The cattle prod clattered against the concrete floors. He tried to scuttle backward away from her. But she sank razor-tipped fingers even deeper into him and stared down into his fear-wide eyes while the pleasure at his helplessness fizzed through her like champagne.

"Get the fuck off me!" he shouted and tried to buck her off him.

But he didn't get to tell her what to do. Shrieking down into his face, Mai slashed her talons across his chest and shredded through his shirt, down through layers of skin. Blood and screams burst out of him, rushing over Mai in an orgiastic flood.

Around her, she suddenly became aware of the other men, one scrambling to open the steel door, the other rushing toward her

FIONA ZEDDE

with his gun. She jumped over her cousin's limp and bleeding body, finding the gun lifting to aim at her.

Everyone except Mai moved slowly.

So slowly that it was nothing for her to grab the gun and disassemble it in the air, the semiautomatic pistol falling in separate pieces away from the hand that held it. The pieces were still falling when Mai reached through the air and cut the big man's throat.

Her body felt warmer than ever before. Cooler air brushed over her skin as she leapt over the dying body for the man fumbling with the heavy door and trying to get out. Mai grabbed him, ignoring his shouts of terror, and slammed him into the steel door. With a crack of sound, the man broke. He crumpled to the floor at Mai's feet.

Then she turned in time to see her cousin teleporting away, a throb of energy in the room warning of his intention just before he began to disappear. She grabbed him and dragged him back into the hard room. Her fingers locked into his shredded shirt, into his skin. His blood erupted under her fingernails.

"Fuck you!" He shouted and jerked under her. "You can't kill me."

He panted and tried to fight her off, but Mai held on. She snarled down at him, wrestling him under her to the ground, knowing she was moving faster than he could see while he thrashed, his gaze dashing into space, looking for her in locations she no longer occupied. He looked terrified, and Mai was gloriously glad.

The pulse throbbed in his throat, a trapped guppy for Mai to rip out. She curled her fingers.

"Stop!" A voice thundered through the room and froze Mai's claws a breath away from Ethan's jugular.

The room shivered again but in a different way, a more subtle ripple of space than when her cousin used his power. A woman stepped out of the wall toward Mai and Ethan. The clothes she wore, an all-black uniform with the red and yellow sunburst insignia of an enforcer, were very familiar. But the woman herself…

"Don't kill him," she said to Mai. Her voice thrummed with Power, echoing in the massive room.

She stopped only a few feet away, her hands held away from her body to show she had no weapons. But they both knew that meant nothing. Her slender but powerful figure radiated power in controlled waves. After a brief hesitation, she pulled the green-tinted goggles from her face, and the eyes that came into view almost undid Mai.

In them, Mai saw her reflection, as clearly as she saw her cousin under her. Her own eyes, narrowed and predatory, were assessing the best way to harm the woman, then get back to the business of killing Ethan. With a rippling of dark-green scales all over her body, slicked wet but drying now, she was no longer in the water. Most of her shirt had torn away to show her black bra and the scaled skin of her belly, superficially torn by her own talons but already healing.

She looked feral. A creature of dark water and violent nightmares. She'd completely transformed. Mai drew a shocked breath but didn't release Ethan.

Because she saw something else in the enforcer, something very familiar despite the masked features and the voice reverberating in the room the way no one else's had.

Under the press of her knees, Ethan moved again, his efforts to teleport away warping the air around his body. But her blood grip on his shoulder was enough to trap him.

The woman slid closer. "Don't do this, Mai." She said her name like they knew each other.

But the only way Mai knew her was from the photos of her work. And, Mai suddenly realized, her unwelcome appearance in Mai's bedroom a few nights ago. She dug her fingers harder into Ethan's shoulder, ripped off a piece of his shirt, and stuffed it into his mouth before he could cry out. She'd heard enough of his bullshit to last a lifetime.

"Why are you holding me back when you're the one who started all this? Isn't this pig's death"—she clenched her fist in Ethan's hair and shook him once—"what you wanted all along?" Mai felt Ethan stiffen under her hand and shout a curse toward the enforcer, but she ignored him. It didn't matter now if he knew this was who'd killed Stephen.

"I may want him dead, but the enforcers need him to live." The woman darted a glance toward the wavering portal she'd just come through. "My team will be here any moment. I wanted to make sure—" She cut herself off with a low curse. "Are you all right?"

Before Mai could respond, the portal shivered, and three uniformed figures stepped into the warehouse, their boots thudding against the cement floor as they fanned out in the room with guns raised. She easily recognized Denali, Ty, and Nuala behind their masks.

How did they…?

Taking advantage of her distraction, the enforcer fell into a crouch beside Mai, bringing the scent of oranges laced with the sweetness of vanilla. Suddenly, the woman's features became as clear as if they weren't covered at all. Mai drew in a shocked breath but said nothing, too aware of the other official-looking figures busy checking on the crumpled bodies around the warehouse.

They didn't know the Absolution Killer was one of them.

Xóchitl.

The woman's name fluttered at the back of her throat, but she swallowed it and swallowed her secret. *Their* secret. And just like that, Mai wasn't ambivalent anymore. Her mind buzzed with everything she knew now about herself and about the enforcer by her side, about everything she thought was possible.

She dropped her gaze to Ethan's and gripped his shoulder again. Her thoughts must have shown on her face, because he bucked in her grip, spitting noises around the gag in his mouth. With a growl of irritation, Xóchitl slapped handcuffs on him, both his wrists and ankles. The cuffs glowed a bright gold and hummed with an invisible force.

With Ethan subdued, Mai relaxed her grip on him. With each breath, she felt her scales and talons receding, her teeth losing their sharp points. His blood remained a brilliant red under her fingernails.

Boots thudded closer, and Mai looked up to see Denali's covered features. "All clear here?" he asked.

Mai jerked her head in a nod, unable to look at Xóchitl with what she was about to do. "I think it's Ethan," she said to Denali, trying to look bruised and properly victimized. Not hard to do with the blood on her face and the shredded clothes hanging off her. "He's the killer you want."

Nuala appeared at Denali's side. "Are you sure?" But she tore into Ethan with her pitiless stare as if she'd caught him stuffing the I CONFESS note down Stephen's throat.

But before Mai could answer, the steel door to the warehouse flew open and slammed into the walls. Her mother surged through it, power rushing from her outstretched palms. Energy swirled around her, and a wild breeze whipped her hair around her face and fluttered back her suit jacket. But she was twenty years too late.

"Mai!"

Mandaia was as close to frantic as Mai had ever seen her. But she stopped as if she'd slammed into an invisible barrier when she saw Mai and Ethan with the enforcers. The very air crackled once, then began to simmer down as she lowered her hands. The breeze she brought with her quieted. Cayman and two of Mandaia's longtime guards rushed into the room behind her. Horror and regret twisted Cayman's face, and he immediately sought Mai's eyes. But she couldn't look at him.

"Mai has done nothing wrong, enforcer," Mandaia said to the woman kneeling next to Mai. Her tone was almost...pleading. "She was only protecting herself." Her eyes swept over Mai and the carnage in the room, the tank with its large red stain and massive crack across the front.

Mai was grateful her brother stayed on the other side of the room and away from her.

"We are well aware of what has been happening." The woman Mai knew as Xóchitl took off her mask and rose to her feet, leaving the handcuffs glowing around Ethan's hands. And even though Mai had already known what face lay under the mask, seeing those familiar features revealed still left her breathless with shock. "The Tribunal of Enforcers asked me to intervene once Ethan Redstone became a suspect in multiple assaults," Xóchitl said. "I've already taken action as a lead commander of the region, and this man must pay for his crimes against the Families."

Mandaia looked surprised. "Against the Families?"

"Yes." Xóchitl looked down at Ethan, who flinched into the floor as if still trying to disappear from the warehouse. "He destroyed and defiled, just like his father did, and helped to hide the evidence of both their crimes by planting false clues." She paused for half a breath, though Mai thought she was the only one to realize it, "and becoming a supposed vigilante killer the humans call Absolution."

Gasps echoed around the room, but Xóchitl continued. "Stephen Redstone preyed primarily on human children, but this one harmed only Meta young, very passive ones or ones with no power."

Mai heard the sound her brother made, as if he was going to be sick, but it seemed to come from far away. Relief seeped into her. Xóchitl was accepting the bloody gift she offered. On the ground, Ethan yanked desperately at his handcuffs and tried to shout denials from behind the gag.

"I- I..." She thought her mother would say she didn't believe any of it, but instead Mandaia cleared her throat and started again. "For how long?"

"Ethan has been active for at least six years," Xóchitl answered. "His father for much, much longer."

Six years. The same amount of time Absolution had been killing for. Mai jerked a look at Xóchitl, but the woman's face was cold and unreadable.

Mandaia smoothed her hands down the front of her suit, easily regaining any lost composure. "I should have known." She stood over Ethan, her high heels within easy striking distance of his face. "But I allowed my brother to turn me away from the truth."

"There are many things you should have known and should have done," Xóchitl said.

THE POWER OF MERCY

Her lips drawn in a thin line, Mandaia looked up. "Like protect my own daughter."

"Exactly."

Mai stumbled to her feet as the two women continued their conversation, not knowing what to think. Her mother's face hardened into familiar, unyielding lines, but her eyes displayed a shocking swirl of emotions.

Xóchitl nodded once, a sharp and unforgiving motion. "Ethan and his *helpers*"—she sneered at Mandaia as she said the word and spared one hard glance at Cayman—"made it seem like you knew the entire time what your brother was doing, and that you helped him get away with it."

Alarm rattled in Mai's chest. He made it *seem* like her mother knew? Mai looked from Xóchitl to her mother, but they stared only at each other.

"Earlier today, my secretary showed me some files, proof of things I'd supposedly helped Stephen hide." Mandaia's hands tightened into fists at her sides. The windows rattled as if a storm were passing through. "That's when I knew."

Xóchitl settled her mask back on her face. "You have some things to set right in your house," she said. "Just as I do."

With a nod from her, the other enforcers stepped forward and yanked Ethan to his feet. "We'll take this one now," Xóchitl said. "If you wish to speak on his behalf—"

"I won't," Mandaia said.

"Very well."

Denali raised a hand, and the wall they'd walked through before rippled. He and the other enforcers walked toward it with Ethan gagged and struggling between them.

"See you another time, Mai," Xóchitl called out softly just before she, too, disappeared.

As soon as the enforcers left, her mother's guards got to work, silently cleaning up the room. One, with fire at her fingertips, incinerated the bodies where they lay, while the other gathered the guns and tools of torture. Mai flinched when the guard picked up the cattle prod. She was too numb to do much more than stare at them, at her brother and mother, who warily watched her in return.

Cayman broke the tense silence. "Mai, I didn't know he'd go this far. I didn't realize—"

"What? You thought he'd only torture me a little bit?"

He flinched and took a step back. Then a familiar look carved his face in stone. "I would've done the same thing if somebody murdered *you*."

"Enough." Mandaia stepped between them and put her back to Cayman. An emotion flickered briefly behind her eyes, like a light going on, then off. "I didn't know," she said.

Mai stared at her in disbelief. "But I told you!" Beyond her control, her voice rose into a high wail. The sound of animal pain. "I told you what he was doing to me."

The past rushed over her in a heaving flood: Mai carried in her mother's arms through Piedmont Park, her fingers lifting to touch the bright-white dogwood blossoms they walked under. The two of them on their backs in the yard, pointing up at the sky and naming the stars.

All mere illusions of safety and affection, all beautiful and cruel lies.

And the worst of it all, being twelve years old and powerless, sobbing as her mother abandoned her to torture and then to Stephen, waiting for a rescue that never came.

"Stephen swore to me it wasn't true," her mother said softly. She blinked at the now-blank wall where Xóchitl had disappeared with Ethan as if it held all the answers to her questions.

Mai staggered back as if Mandaia had actually struck her. Then she swallowed thickly and shook her head. "It's fine!" Her voice cracked through the air like a whip. "It doesn't matter now."

But her mother didn't seem the least bit impressed or intimidated by her outburst. She stepped closer, a hand on Mai's elbow. "At least let me take care of you now. It shouldn't be like this between us."

The difference between the woman she had known most of her life and the stranger who stood before her was too much for Mai to bear. Then she realized what was different. *She* was different. She had power now, and now her mother wanted to mother her. She straightened and pulled away from Mandaia, ignoring the pain that ignited through her body.

"Things are the same as they've always been," she said.

Then she left the warehouse under her own power, not expecting her mother to follow.

CHAPTER 11

ALMOST SIX WEEKS PASSED BEFORE Mai saw Xóchitl again. A colleague took over her classes after the university issued a statement about her having some sort of family emergency. Mai rolled her eyes when she heard. *She'd* been the one with a real family emergency, but that didn't stop her from going to work.

But so much time passed, she thought she'd never see Xóchitl again. Although Denali and the others must have known where she was, Mai didn't feel right asking them anything. Mai didn't want any suspicion to fall on Xóchitl's head just because she couldn't keep her sadness, or her curiosity, to herself. And so she stayed quiet and wondered. Until the morning she received an e-mail, along with a plane ticket to Mexico.

I'll tell you everything, the e-mail said.

Mai had never been able to resist the lure of answered questions.

She'd been to Mexico at least a dozen times before, mostly for academic conferences and once for spring break, enough that she spoke decent Spanish and knew how to get around the country. But the place Xóchitl's directions guided her to was as foreign to her as the Nahuatl language two women were speaking as she got out of the taxi and approached the large, yellow house.

On the Caribbean side of the country now, Mai felt like she was in a postcard, with the swaying palm trees, purple and yellow hibiscus lining the walkway, and the intrigued toucans perched on the low trees overhead.

On the wide verandah of the house, two women sat shelling peas and exchanging laughter between their words, barely stopping their beautiful rhythm when Mai approached, although the taxi pulling up and then away from the gate must have been sign enough of her presence.

"Good afternoon," she greeted the women with a wave. "Can you tell me where Xóchitl is?"

The woman on the left, older and with her short hair sprinkled with tiny pink flowers, laughed at Mai, maybe at her pronunciation of Xóchitl's name, and made a *welcome* gesture with the hand not busy holding the wide, silver bowl in her lap. "She's inside. Follow the music to the kitchen."

"She's expecting you," said the other, also beautiful but with a tower of silver hair.

Mai thanked them and made sure to wipe her sandaled feet before stepping onto the verandah. The house wasn't small, but it was nowhere as massive as Mandaia's mansion. Once inside, she heard the faint echoes of far-off conversations.

It didn't take her long to find Xóchitl. She sat in a pool of sunlight at the kitchen table and slowly ate from a bowl of sliced mangoes while staring off into space. Tejano music played softly from the radio. A sea-scented breeze slid in through the open windows.

Mai caught her breath. Xóchitl looked like a completely different person from the enforcer she saw last. Or the professor she'd known first. A yellow sarong tied behind her neck left her shoulders bare and highlighted the glowing deep gold of her skin. Her short coils were wilder, gleaming from a recent shampoo and some sort of oil. In the kitchen of her house on the Caribbean coast of Mexico, Xóchitl chose to look harmless, a beautiful woman surrounded by color and warmth. But she didn't hide the hum of Power radiating from her, an electric crackle in the air that brushed against Mai's skin and seduced her closer.

When Mai had thought about this moment—and she'd had a long enough time between the six weeks in Atlanta and the three hours on the plane—she imagined letting loose her own anger, her accusations of betrayal—*how could you sleep with me to get the information you wanted?*—and even indifference. But she never thought she'd feel this overwhelming sense of…relief. Xóchitl was in her own home, not taken away by the enforcers as Ethan had been. She was free. She was safe.

"You came." Xóchitl put down her fork, surprise in her voice.

"The women outside said you were expecting me."

"I was hopeful." She smiled briefly and gestured to the fruit. "Would you like some?"

"No, thank you." *I'd rather watch you eat.* "All I want right now is answers." Mai took the empty seat across from her and dropped her small bag under the table. An irrepressible fountain of gladness bubbled up inside her.

"And that's all you came here for?" Amusement shimmered in Xóchitl's dark eyes.

Mai would rather bite off her tongue than confess she'd been dreaming about Xóchitl for weeks now, wondering where she was, waking up in the middle of the night and gasping her name. "Answers would be a good start," she said.

The last few weeks had been frightening for her, a time of change and of wondering in what direction she should now take her life. She finally took her sister's advice and started seeing a therapist. But she still wasn't ready to deal with the new version of her mother who wanted to be in her company, who asked questions instead of issuing orders. Who talked about loving Mai and wanting to protect her.

Mai couldn't help but think her new manifestation of Power had something to do with her mother's sudden desire for a better relationship. She wasn't as weak as her mother had thought, so now she was actually worthy of respect and warmth.

Mandaia insisted, though, that Mai had been the one to pull away first all those years ago, railing and cursing at the family until they finally gave in and sent her away to boarding school and away from Stephen. Too late.

They both had a long way to go. And speaking of which…

"So. An explanation?" Mai prodded Xóchitl, who gave that nonsmile of hers again.

"I think you already know everything." She tilted her head, and the sun fell across her face, turning one brown eye into molten gold.

"But I'd like you to spell it out for me so I'm not operating purely on assumptions."

The truth was, Mai only had guesses about what had happened to bring Xóchitl to Atlanta. Why she ended up teaching at the university. Why she deliberately antagonized Mai, seduced her, and then stopped her from killing her cousin.

"Six years ago, Ethan killed my sister in San Miguel de Allende."

Mai nearly choked on her next breath. That wasn't what she expected.

"Ixchel was Powerless. She was staying with her human mother at the time." Xóchitl, her voice leeched of all inflection, speared a piece of mango with the fork but didn't eat it. "Everyone knew Ethan Redstone did it. But even as an enforcer, I couldn't touch him." Xóchitl's hand tightened around the fork. When she seemed to realize what she was doing, she abandoned it in the bowl with a clang of stainless steel against ceramic. "His family—your family—was too powerful. He was too careful."

"Because I couldn't kill him, I killed someone else. Another predator. But it didn't feel like I changed anything, so I killed another, then more." She finally met Mai's gaze, and the pain Mai saw there made her chest hurt. "It wasn't going to end. My grief for my sister. My powerlessness." Xóchitl curled her fingers into loose fists on the tabletop. "I saw myself on that hamster wheel for the rest of my life, taking out substitutes while the man who'd fractured my family carried on like usual, all because his father protected him."

"So you got rid of his father."

"I got rid of his father," Xóchitl confirmed. "He was my hardest kill." She bared her sharp teeth. "But the most satisfying."

"Why? Because it brought you to Ethan?"

"Yes." Xóchitl's voice was like a flash of lightning in the room. Powerful and sure. "And it brought me to you."

The words washed over Mai like a heated caress. They were what she wanted to hear, but did they mean anything? She'd spent so much of her life being unwanted and unloved that she *needed* to hear it all.

"Tell me," she whispered.

Xóchitl didn't need any more prompting than that. "You took revenge on the people who made your life hell by saving humans and caring for your own needs, instead of becoming filled with poison. That's what surprised me when I found you. Seeing you with your ideals and your drive to make a difference made me want to be a better person." Xóchitl's eyes lightened again. "And then I just wanted to fuck you."

Mai blushed. "You did do that."

"And I want to do it again." There was a fierce sensuality to the look Xóchitl turned on her, voracious and volatile, her face fully in the sun now and her eyes molten enough to burn through to Mai's very core.

Mai should have been frightened. She should have wanted to run. But this sign of Xóchitl's force only made her more certain of where she wanted to be. This woman knew her and still wanted to stay. She knew about Stephen's abuse, that her own cousin had tried to kill her. She knew about Mercy.

Still, Mai hesitated. "And what about what you said before, about wanting to know me? Do you still mean it?"

"Yes," Xóchitl said. Her gaze was unwavering.

Mai took a trembling breath and looked away. Xóchitl was strong. She was the kind of warrior and protector Mai wished she'd had as a child growing up in a household that failed to keep her safe.

"If you want me, you can have me now."

Mai startled. It occurred to her suddenly that she hadn't known until now what Xóchitl's power was. "Get out of my mind," she said.

"I'm not in your mind, at least not right now. I don't need to be. You're as transparent as your pretty blouse." She waved a hand at the pink camisole Mai wore with her white linen pants. "You're not even trying to hide what you're thinking."

It was true. She was tired of hiding. And though she might have fooled herself into thinking she was coming to visit Xóchitl for answers, she was actually on her doorstep to be herself, to take off all the masks they'd both worn and finally lay them aside.

"Let me be that for you," Xóchitl said, her voice low and throbbing with tender emotion. An echo of her words slid into Mai's mind like the most intimate of caresses. "Let me be *your* Mercy." She left her chair to walk toward Mai, the sarong swaying on her body with each step, her scent wrapping Mai in comforting notes of citrus and spice.

Mai shook her head, but she was already leaning back into the arms encircling her from behind, into the steady warmth she'd once mistaken for cold. She melted into Xóchitl and felt like she'd traveled a very long way to end up at home. Finally.

ABOUT FIONA ZEDDE

Jamaican-born Fiona Zedde currently lives and writes in Atlanta, Georgia. She is the author of several novellas and novels of lesbian love and desire, including the Lambda Literary Award finalists, *Bliss* and *Every Dark Desire*. Her novel, *Dangerous Pleasures*, was winner of the About.com Readers' Choice Award for Best Lesbian Novel or Memoir of 2012.

Her short fiction has appeared in various anthologies including the Cleis Press Best Lesbian Erotica series, *Wicked: Sexy Tales of Legendary Lovers*, *Iridescence: Sensuous Shades of Lesbian Erotica*, and *Fist of the Spider Woman*.

CONNECT WITH FIONA
Website: www.fionazedde.com
E-Mail: f.zedde@gmail.com

OTHER BOOKS FROM YLVA PUBLISHING

www.ylva-publishing.com

SHATTERED
Lee Winter

ISBN: 978-3-95533-563-2
Length: 194 pages (69,000 words)

Shattergirl, Earth's first lesbian guardian is refusing to save people and has gone off the grid. Lena Martin, the street-smart tracker with a silver tongue and a disdain for the rogue guardians she chases, has only days to bring her home. As the pair clash heatedly, masks begin to crack and brutal secrets are exposed that could shatter them both.

EX-WIVES OF DRACULA
Georgette Kaplan

ISBN: 978-3-95533-410-9
Length: 338 pages (122,000 words)

Mindy's best friend, Lucia, is a vampire. Every second Mindy spends with her she's in danger of becoming dinner. But Lucia needs help. To keep her alive they need fresh blood, and to cure her they have to kill her sire. So why is it that Nosferatu, the cops, and the chance of becoming an unwilling blood donor don't scare Mindy half as much as the way she feels when Lucia looks at her?

BETWEEN THE LINES

(Cops and Docs – Book 3)

KD Williamson

ISBN: 978-3-95533-825-1
Length: 370 pages (118,000 words)

Cool, detached psychiatrist Tonya Preston prefers dealing with her patients more than her family. When her path dramatically crosses that of irrepressible rookie cop Haley Jordan, she's thrown out of her comfort zone. A simmering attraction draws them close. But will it be enough when work, family and a confronting police case start to tear at them?

PIECES

G Benson

ISBN: 978-3-95533-805-3
Length: 292 pages (104,000 words)

Carmen is sixteen, homeless, and desperate to keep her and her kid brother out of foster care. Ollie, also sixteen, has a life that's all about parents, school pressure, and friends. One kiss changes everything. Ollie is captivated, but Carmen vanishes. When they cross paths later, everything is different.

A young-adult, queer romance about what we're prepared to sacrifice for those we care about.

The Power of Mercy
© 2017 by Fiona Zedde

ISBN: 978-3-95533-854-1

Also available as e-book.

Published by Ylva Publishing, legal entity of Ylva Verlag, e.Kfr.
Ylva Verlag, e.Kfr.
Owner: Astrid Ohletz
Am Kirschgarten 2
65830 Kriftel
Germany

www.ylva-publishing.com

First edition: 2017

Credits
Edited by Gill McKnight and Michelle Aguilar
Proofread by Paulette Callen
Cover Design and Print Layout by Streetlight Graphics